ATHLETE vs. MATHLETE

DOUBLE DRIBBLE

ALSO BY W. C. MACK

Athlete vs. Mathlete

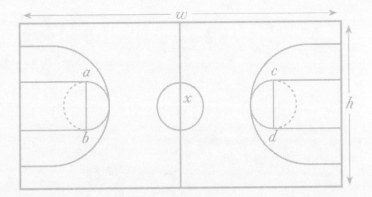

ATHLETE vs. MATHLETE

DOUBLE DRIBBLE

W. C. Mack

BLOOMSBURY

NEW YORK   LONDON   NEW DELHI   SYDNEY

First published in the United States of America in November 2013
by Bloomsbury Children's Books
www.bloomsbury.com

For information about permission to reproduce selections from this book, write to
Permissions, Bloomsbury Children's Books, 1385 Broadway, New York, New York 10018
Bloomsbury books may be purchased for business or promotional use. For information on bulk
purchases please contact Macmillan Corporate and Premium Sales Department at specialmarkets@
macmillan.com

Library of Congress Cataloging-in-Publication Data
Mack, W. C.
Athlete vs. mathlete : double dribble / by W. C. Mack. — First U.S. edition.
pages   cm
Summary: Fraternal twins Russ and Owen's domination of the seventh-grade basketball team
falters when Mitch and Marcus Matthews, identical twins, arrive and prove their skill on the court
and in the classroom.
ISBN 978-1-59990-938-7 (paperback) • ISBN 978-1-61963-129-8 (hardcover)
ISBN 978-1-61963-150-2 (e-book)
[1. Twins—Fiction.   2. Brothers—Fiction.   3. Basketball—Fiction.   4. Competition
(Psychology)—Fiction.   5. Schools—Fiction.]   I. Title.   II. Title: Athlete versus mathlete,
double dribble.   III. Title: Double dribble.
PZ7.M18996Atf 2013   [Fic]—dc23   2013004314

Book design by Nicole Gastonguay
Typeset by Westchester Book Composition
Printed and bound in the U.S.A. by Thomson-Shore Inc., Dexter, Michigan
2 4 6 8 10 9 7 5 3 1 (paperback)
2 4 6 8 10 9 7 5 3 1 (hardcover)

All papers used by Bloomsbury Publishing, Inc., are natural, recyclable products
made from wood grown in well-managed forests. The manufacturing processes
conform to the environmental regulations of the country of origin.

For my brother, Ian McDonald,
who always smoked me at driveway basketball

And for Mike Smith, who wishes he were still
shooting hoops for the Estacada Tigers

ATHLETE vs. MATHLETE

OWEN

Starting Lineup

The Woodlawn Wildcats were going down!

But not without a fight, it turned out.

It was late in the fourth quarter and my socks were so soaked with sweat, I felt like I was standing in the shallow end of a swimming pool instead of Woodlawn's gym.

My best friend, Chris, dribbled down the court and passed to Nate, the fastest guy on our team.

Nate took off, chased by a bunch of green and yellow uniforms, and dodged one of their guards with a couple of awesome moves that could have been ESPN highlights (if ESPN covered middle-school basketball).

The crowd was on its feet.

But then Nate was stuck dealing with Woodlawn's other guard, who wouldn't budge.

I watched my teammate try to work some magic, but he kept getting blocked by the guard's long, skinny arms.

"That guy's a freakin' octopus," I said to Chris.

He nodded. "We've gotta help Nate out."

I tried to get open by ditching the big Wildcat who'd been stuck to me like a brand-new Band-Aid for the whole game. The kid seemed to know every move I was going to make before *I* did. When I broke left, he was already there. If I went right, his freckled face and hot ketchup breath were waiting for me. I seriously couldn't get away from him, no matter what.

But luckily, I wasn't the only Lewis and Clark Pioneer out there.

"I'm open!" Paul shouted, and I watched Nate throw the ball right to him.

A perfect pass.

Perfect teamwork.

I rested my hands on my knees, catching my breath while Paul dribbled a couple of times and checked out his options.

He didn't have too many.

"Shoot!" The crowd yelled so loud I thought the backboard would shatter.

The Woodlawn cheerleaders started jumping up and down, screaming about "spirit" to distract him.

But Paul had two little sisters who were even more annoying than the cheerleaders, so he just smiled and got into position. In about two seconds, the ball was in the air again.

I willed it to go straight into the basket.

And it *did*, dropping through the net with a big, fat *swish*.

"Sweet!" I cried over the cheers of our fans. I high-fived Paul and Nicky Chu, who were as amped as I was.

We had only two minutes left and we were still down by three points, but there was hope. Lots of it.

Coach pulled Paul out and it was Russ's turn to hit the hardwood. My twin yanked up his blue-and-white shorts so the tucked-in jersey I kept telling him wasn't cool was even more obvious.

Some things never change.

I nodded at Russ and he smiled back with a flash of his braces. Then he bent to retie the laces of the most awesome Nikes on the planet.

The next thing I knew, he was doing some stretch I'd never seen before, his elbows sticking out all over the place. It wasn't anything we'd been taught, which meant Russ probably read about it in a yoga book or something.

As I watched him, I was still kind of weirded out by how comfortable my brainiac brother looked on the court. After years of science fairs and nerd herds, he'd taken a chance on basketball and it had totally paid off.

Sure, his dribbling still needed work and he wasn't exactly the fastest guy on the team, but he had the third-best shooting percentage and his fan base was out of control.

"Let's see some hustle, Russell!" some eighth-grade girls shrieked from the stands, proving the point.

My brother's face turned bright pink.

The ref blew his whistle and Chris passed the ball to me.

I could hear the Wildcat behind me breathing hard, and I'm pretty sure he sprayed the back of my neck with ketchup spit.

I pivoted right, and by some kind of fluke he didn't see that move coming.

With nothing but open court in front of me, I could finally *do* something!

"Shoot!" the crowd yelled.

But I wasn't going to rush anything. We had time on the clock, so there was no reason to waste the shot. With all the eyes in the gym on me, I took a couple of deep breaths.

When I was ready, I dribbled a little closer to the net. I stopped to bounce the ball one more time, then let it fly.

And man, did it soar!

I couldn't hear a sound as I watched the ball shoot through the air. When it found its target, it wobbled around the rim in slow motion for a second or two before finally falling through the net.

Yes!

Two points for Owen Evans, thank you very much!

I jogged back toward center court.

Being so close to a win that we could taste it was nothing

new. After all, the Pioneers had been rocking a winning streak lately.

Okay, we'd won only two games in a row, but streaks have to start somewhere, right?

We'd smoked Roseglen by eighteen points, which was our biggest lead ever. But the Lincoln game had been more of a nail-biter, and we'd only won by six.

Now we had less than a minute left before the final buzzer and we were down a single point.

I could tell the whole team was feeling the pressure.

Nicky Chu was biting his lip so hard, I was pretty sure I saw blood on his chin.

Paul was cracking his knuckles fast enough that it sounded like he'd just added milk to a bowl of Rice Krispies.

Russ was mumbling something about the periodic table, which he only did when he was wigging out.

And me? I was watching the seconds on the clock tick by at double their usual speed.

Lucky for us, Russ got fouled about half a second later by a kid who'd been on the ref's radar since the tip-off.

I watched my brother walk up to the line, his blue-and-silver Nikes squeaking against the hardwood. He adjusted his glasses, which was another sign he was stressed, and licked his lips.

I watched him roll his shoulders like he'd seen Carl Walters do during Blazer games. Then he dropped the ball for the first of his usual three bounces.

It hit the toe of his shoe and shot out of bounds.

"Calm down, Russ," I whispered, as the skin on the back of his neck turned bright red.

The ref tossed the ball back to him, and he bounced it three times with no problems.

The whole gym was dead quiet as he bent his bony knees, then straightened up to take the shot.

The ball seemed to hang in the air for about a year, but in reality it was barely long enough for me to blink.

I held my breath and then let it out in a big "Yes!" when it hit the backboard and dropped through the net.

The handful of Pioneers fans who made the trip with us cheered as loudly as they could.

We were tied!

The ref tossed the ball back to Russ, who went through his little pre-throw ritual again. Glasses adjusted, lips licked, shoulders rolled, then three bounces.

I couldn't help crossing my fingers as he took the second shot. All we needed was one stinkin' basket to take the win!

Russ threw the ball.

His arc was perfect, his speed looked good, and the next thing I knew, he'd sunk it.

We won!

I was the first guy to run over and slap him on the back. A month ago, I would have been totally jealous that he'd won the game for us, but Russ and I had worked things out, on and off the court.

Instead of seeing that final shot as a moment of glory he'd stolen from me, I saw it for what it really was: the point we needed, right when we needed it, scored by an awesome teammate.

By the time the final buzzer sounded, the Pioneers were already celebrating the win by jumping around, high-fiving, and slapping each other on the back.

Coach Baxter looked as happy about the three-game streak as we were.

The rest of the guys and I got in line to thank the Wildcats, shaking hands with each of them. Mr. Ketchup wouldn't even look at me, but I thanked him, anyway. It's called good sportsmanship, and even though I didn't always show mine, I was working on it.

Coach pulled us into a huddle and his smile was huge.

"I like what I'm seeing out there, Pioneers," he said. "You guys are really coming together as a team. Your passing game is improving and your communication is a hundred percent better than it used to be. Good job, men."

I was smiling when I headed for the shower. Coach was the only person on the planet who called us men.

The visitors' locker room was loud and rowdy when I got in there, with everybody shouting stuff like "Three for three!" and "That was *awesome!*"

When I was showered and dressed, I shoved my sweaty uniform into my blue-and-white team gym bag.

"Good game, Owen," Russ said, reaching into the locker next to mine for his regular clothes.

"You, too," I told him, dropping onto the bench to wait for the rest of the guys.

"Chris was just talking about play-offs. Do you think we could really make it?" he asked, as his head got stuck in his turtleneck.

I waited for his face to pop out again.

"It's still early in the season," I told him. "But yeah. Totally."

Coming up on our schedule was Hogarth Middle School, which was guaranteed to be a tough game. The Huskies were no joke, mostly because of their star player, Dante Powers. I'd never gone up against him before, but he was a freakin' legend. He was the first seventh grader in the state of Oregon to score over thirty points in a single game.

In a single game!

My record was twenty points, but I was working on that, too.

I sometimes wondered what it would be like to be Dante Powers. Everybody knew his name. Everybody knew his record.

Everybody wanted to beat him.

I was pretty sure he'd have a Nike shoe named after him by the time he graduated from high school. And no matter how awesome they were, I wouldn't buy a pair, because he'd always be a Hogarth Huskie to me.

He'd probably go straight from twelfth grade to the NBA, like Kobe Bryant or LeBron James. And then my mom would probably tell me that college is more important than basketball, which it isn't. Except to her and Russ, anyway.

As the Hogarth game got closer, I couldn't stop thinking about what was going to happen in that Huskies gym.

If the Pioneers beat them, it wouldn't matter how fast Dante Powers got drafted or how many millions of dollars his first contract was for, because I, Owen Evans, would be able to spend the rest of my life telling people that my team had taken him down.

And that legendary victory would happen in just three weeks.

I met up with most of my teammates in the Lewis and Clark cafeteria the next afternoon, after the most boring English class ever.

"Hot-dog day," I groaned as I read the chalkboard on the far wall.

The place smelled worse than the wet socks I'd peeled off after last night's game. I had no idea what kind of mad scientists the cafeteria ladies were, but they had some serious gross-out skills. And it was pretty much guaranteed that if the lunch special smelled that bad, it would look even worse.

"Skipping the dogs?" Nicky Chu asked when I sat down next to him at our usual table.

"No doubt." I shook my head. "How do you ruin wieners, anyway? All you have to do is boil them."

"Maybe they're boiling them in acid," he suggested, "or toxic waste." He shrugged as he bit into a ham-and-cheese sandwich.

I unwrapped my own turkey and sprouts, wishing Mom would switch back to lettuce so it wouldn't look like I was eating boogers all the time.

I checked out the Masters of the Mind table, where Russ and his buddies looked all excited. They were probably figuring out the scientific name for peanut butter or something.

Just then, a slice of pink meat came flying through the air. When it landed next to Paul's juice box, it sounded like a wet slap.

"Really?" He sighed, pushing it out of the way with his math textbook. "I mean, *really*?"

"That's just wrong," I said, shaking my head as I bit into my sandwich.

We didn't bother looking to see who'd launched the meat, since it always came from the same place: the eighth graders' table.

I couldn't wait until next year, when we were the big kids and all those jerks were freshmen at the high school.

I wished I could be there to see *them* dodging lunch meat on their first day. I was pretty sure seniors could whip a bologna bomb harder and faster than any of them could.

"Did you hear?" Chris asked, dropping a tray with two nuclear hot dogs on the table and sitting down across from me.

"Hear what?" I asked, trying to fan the stink away with my hand.

"About the new kids," he said, tearing open a package of mustard and squeezing it all over his lunch.

It was going to take a lot more than mustard to fix that steaming pile.

"What new kids?" Paul asked.

"*What new kids?*" Chris repeated, obviously loving the fact that he had the scoop for once. "The ones Coach Baxter just handed Pioneers jerseys and welcomed to the team." He looked around the table. "And by that, I mean *our* team."

"What?" Nicky gasped.

"No way," Paul said, shaking his head.

"I'm serious. We have two new teammates."

"Impossible," Paul said. "Nobody makes the Pioneers without trying out." He looked from me to Nate to Nicky Chu. "We *all* had to."

"Nope. This is different," Chris told him. "They're transfer students."

"From where?" Nate asked.

"Minnesota," he said, like that was supposed to impress us.

"So?" we all asked at the same time.

"So, they're freakin' awesome," Chris said, grinning.

Freakin' awesome transfer students from Minnesota who didn't have to try out? I couldn't find a single piece of that description I liked. I took another bite of my sandwich and wondered what was going on.

"How do you know they're awesome?" Paul asked.

"Yeah," Nate said. "Did you see them play?"

Chris shrugged. "No, but they look like they're already in high school."

"That doesn't mean they're good," Nicky Chu argued.

"I'm talking letterman jackets, you guys." Chris grinned. "With patches for basketball."

I would have loved my own letterman jacket!

"Hold on," Paul said. "They both showed up wearing letterman jackets?"

"Yeah," Chris said, and nodded.

"*Matching* jackets?" Paul snorted. "Are you kidding me?"

"They dressed like twins on their first day of school?" Nicky Chu shook his head. "Bad idea."

"Lame," Nate agreed.

"No, no. You don't get it," Chris said. "They *are* twins."

"Really?" I asked, wiping some stray sprouts off my chin.

"Yeah," he said, glancing at me. "Like, *real* ones."

Compatible Numbers

When Owen told me about my new teammates, I wasn't worried about their size, their letterman jackets, or the fact that they didn't have to suffer through the grueling tryouts the rest of us Pioneers had (in my case, barely) survived.

What bothered me was that Chris had called them "real" twins.

Real twins.

Owen and I might not have looked or acted even slightly alike, but we'd most definitely been squeezed together for nine months in our mother's belly, and we were born only a few minutes apart.

We'd spent our entire lives sharing birthday parties (though not the same number of guests—he's much more popular than I am), Christmas presents (I don't remember asking for a *Sports Illustrated* subscription, but we'd been "enjoying" one for the past four years); and we'd even shared a bedroom in our old house. I took the top bunk, to be closer to the stars, while Owen took the bottom, to be closer to the bathroom.

And since we'd always been the only set of twins at Lewis and Clark Middle School, it hadn't mattered that we didn't look or act the same. As far as the other students were concerned, we were *the* twins.

So, if the perfectly coordinated new transfer students were "real" twins, what did that make us?

Fake?

Even though I hadn't been there when Chris made the comment, I heard it in my head repeatedly for the rest of the day. It bothered me through two of my favorite classes and during the walk to Nitu's house for a Masters of the Mind meeting.

Real twins.

What was that supposed to mean?

"You know, Russell," Nitu said, when I told her about Chris's comment, "I don't think he meant anything by it."

"I know," I told her, trying to shake off my irritation the same way Pioneers shook things off on the court. "It just hit a nerve."

"Why?"

"I don't know," I admitted with a shrug. "I guess I liked

us being the only set of twins at school. And you know I can't help that Owen and I don't look alike."

Nitu smiled at me, then rhymed, "Basketball is only a game, and twins don't *have* to look the same."

I couldn't help smiling back. I loved rhyming with my Masters teammates, and she was right, too. I was probably being a bit uptight, considering I hadn't even met the new twins yet. I thought for a couple of seconds before rhyming back, "The Pioneers are like my brothers, but I should be willing to welcome others."

"See? That's the spirit," she said, grinning.

We walked past the elementary school, which seemed to have shrunk in the past couple of years. The fireman's pole I'd always been too scared to slide down looked tiny.

"See that little drinking fountain?" I rhymed. "I used to climb it like a mountain."

She laughed and pointed to the playground. "Whenever I fell off those swings, I wished that I could grow some wings."

"Did you really?" I asked, laughing.

"Fall or wish I had wings?" She shook her head. "It doesn't matter. I actually did both."

I didn't remember spending much time in the playground back in those days. While Owen and his friends turned sticks into guns and chased each other at recess and lunch, I spent most of my free time in the library.

What I *did* remember about elementary school was

standing on the stage to accept the Science Award three years in a row. And the Top Student Award twice. Of course, Nitu had won the math honor four times.

"Hey, if these new guys are identical twins," she said, interrupting my thoughts, "do you think they can read each other's minds?"

I laughed. "I doubt it. Telepathy seems a bit—"

"Sci-fi?" she asked.

"I was going to say unlikely," I told her.

She shrugged. "Well, *I* think it would be pretty cool."

I thought about it for a moment. "I don't know about that."

"Why not? Imagine if you didn't have to open your mouth or write anything down because other people knew exactly what you wanted to say."

"But how would you stop them from knowing the things you *didn't* want to say? Or didn't want anyone to know?"

She frowned. "*Hmm.* Good point."

"Our thoughts are the only things in the world that are completely private."

She raised an eyebrow at me. "Wait a second. Are you afraid someone would steal your Masters of the Mind ideas or cheat on a test, using your brain?"

"Well . . . yes." I had a lot of other concerns, too, but those were near the top of the list.

"Oh, Russell," she said. "You're such a worrywart."

I'd been called worse.

In fact, my own brother had recently called me "geek of the week" in the heat of an argument.

But we were past all that. We were past a lot of things, and it felt good to be starting over with Owen. That was part of the reason I was upset about the "real twins" comment. Basketball was a new bond between my brother and me, and it seemed like such a delicate balance, I didn't want anything to change it.

Since I'd joined the Pioneers, the only thing that had been a bit tricky was splitting my time between my Masters of the Mind and basketball teammates. Sometimes I liked to eat lunch with Nitu, Jason, and Sara, but other days I liked being part of the action at the jock table with Owen and the rest of the guys. The conversation wasn't quite as sophisticated, but the guys were a lot of fun.

"I wonder how these new twins are going to fit in at Lewis and Clark," I said to Nitu as we turned into her driveway.

"What do you mean?" she asked. "If they're jocks, they'll just fit in with the jocks, won't they?"

I nodded.

But what if they were a better fit at the jock table than I was? What if letterman jackets were more important than I thought? What if they took over as the school twins *and* took over my spot at the Pioneers table? Where would that leave me?

"Man, you guys look serious," Jason said when he and Sara joined me and Nitu a few minutes later in her basement.

I explained the twin situation to him. "I just feel weird about it."

"That's cool," he said, nodding. "But you know it's going to take more than a couple of new kids to replace you at Lewis and Clark, right, Russ?"

"Uh—"

"Dude, you're an athlete and a mathlete. It sounds like those guys are just a couple of jocks who like to dress the same."

He had a point there. I had pretty well cornered the market on brains and, well, not *brawn*, but athleticism at school.

"You're one of a kind, Russ," Sara said quietly. "Don't give it another thought."

And I didn't. For a while, anyway.

✖ ➗ ➕

By the time the meeting was over, the Masters team still hadn't decided who should become our fifth and final member. It was proving to be a huge challenge.

My stomach growled all the way home, so when I got there, I was thrilled to see Mom in the kitchen making spaghetti.

"Oh, good. You're back. Can you tell your brother we're almost ready?" she asked, licking a bit of sauce from her thumb. "It's his turn to set the table."

"I can set it," I offered.

Mom shook her head. "Changing the chore schedule will only lead to disaster."

She was probably right.

I climbed the stairs and walked into Owen's room. He was sitting at his desk, staring intently at the notebook in front of him. His tongue was sticking out of the corner of his mouth, which meant he was deep in concentration.

"What are you doing?" I asked.

He practically jumped out of his chair.

"Whoa! You scared me, Russ," he said, rubbing his chest like I'd given him a heart attack.

He'd always been a little overdramatic.

"I didn't mean to," I told him, glancing at the notebook. I could make out two figures, one wearing a jersey with an "H" on it, cowering under a basketball hoop while the other slam-dunked a ball.

It didn't take a genius to know that the "H" stood for Hogarth.

"Is that Dante Powers?"

"Yeah. I'm just—"

"Fantasizing about beating him?" I asked, smiling.

"Well . . . yeah."

"Do you think we can do it?" Judging by what I'd heard from the rest of the Pioneers, Dante Powers was a force to be reckoned with.

"As long as we work together," Owen said, having learned some valuable lessons about teamwork recently.

The whole team was working together, and that was the reason for our latest wins.

How would two new players affect the chemistry the rest of us had together?

"Do you think Coach Baxter will play those Minnesota twins right away?" I asked.

Owen laughed. "Wrong sport."

"What?" I asked, confused.

"The Minnesota Twins? They're a baseball team, Russ. Major league baseball."

"Oh. Cool," I said, trying to shrug it off. Flipping through those *Sports Illustrated* magazines every now and then might be a good idea.

"Anyway," Owen continued, "I don't know what Coach will do. Brand-new guys won't know our plays or anything."

"Sure," I said, wincing. I barely knew them myself.

"Hey, are you watching the Blazer game with Dad and me tonight?"

"Who are they playing?" I asked, liking the fact that the answer would actually mean something to me.

"Oklahoma."

A decent team with a higher than average number of fouls. "Sure, I'll watch," I told him, starting to look forward to it.

Ever since I'd joined the Pioneers, Dad had been inviting me to watch the games. It took me a little while to get into it, but once I'd learned the terms and read some background on the team and their players, it had turned into a lot of fun. I liked hanging out on the couch as one of the guys, cheering on *our* team.

When we sat down that night, I got my favorite spot on the middle cushion. That meant I had the best view *and* got to hold the popcorn bowl. It didn't get much better than that.

As soon as the game started, Dad said, "They look ready to win."

"Fire in their eyes," Owen agreed, shoving a handful of popcorn into his mouth.

"They have a better record than Oklahoma," I said, glad to have something to contribute.

"Okay, almost *everyone* has a better record than Oklahoma," Owen said, through his mouthful.

Our relationship might have changed in the last month, but he still liked to be a bit of a basketball know-it-all.

I let it go.

The Blazers played well in the first quarter, but when the second started, things seemed to go downhill. The passes were sloppy, they were taking shots they shouldn't have even considered, and no one looked like they were playing in the same game, let alone on the same team.

"Pass it to Johnson!" Owen shouted at the TV when Lamar Otis threw the ball to Kevin Maple. "Maple's been shooting nothing but bricks!"

I watched as Maple missed another basket.

"You've got to be kidding me," Owen complained. "Johnson was wide open." He flopped against his cushion like it was the most disappointing thing he'd ever seen.

I didn't take it quite so hard. I might have become a fan, but I wasn't a *superfan* yet.

Dad winked at me and I smiled back, then reached for more popcorn.

By the end of the first half, the Blazers had gotten their act together and Owen's enthusiasm had returned.

But in the beginning of the third, Maple was still missing shots and the Blazers were down by twelve points.

"Take the guy out," Owen pleaded. "Put in Marshall, Buckman, Lewis, or . . . *anybody.*"

"They have to give Maple a chance," Dad said. "They paid a lot of money for him."

"How much?" I asked.

"Too much," Owen replied.

"How much is that?" I asked.

"Anything over a dollar would have been too much, and they're giving that guy millions."

"Over the next three years," Dad reminded him.

"Yeah, well, he'll destroy the team in three years," Owen said. "The Rose Garden won't even be standing when his contract is up."

"That seems a little over the top," Dad said, laughing.

"I'm serious," Owen said. "He's the worst thing that could have happened to this team."

But by the fourth quarter, he'd changed his tune.

Maple started making shots. And not just any shots either. He was hitting three-pointers from every possible angle, and every time the ball left his hands I could tell something magical was about to happen.

It took me a few minutes to figure out what was different in that final quarter.

It was Adam Donaldson. The new guy had finally been pulled off the bench and into his first professional game.

"He's from Duke," Owen told me when I asked about him.

Last month, all I would have known was that they were a private research university, but since I'd joined the Pioneers, I'd heard all about their famous basketball program.

I thought about that for a minute. "Didn't Kevin Maple play at Duke?" I asked.

"What?" Owen asked, his attention on the TV. Then he nodded and said, "Yeah. Yeah, they played there together for three years."

For the final few minutes of the game, I didn't watch the ball or the baskets. I watched Maple and Donaldson feed each other the ball, like each knew exactly where the other was at all times. They passed and scored to help the Blazers win the game by twenty-two points.

It was easily the best teamwork I'd ever seen.

Over the Limit

I went to bed that night still smiling about the Blazer game. My favorite NBA team was in the middle of a winning streak, just like we were.

We'd been working so well together lately I'd been feeling like nothing could stop us.

But right before I fell asleep, Russ stopped by my room.

"I'm worried about the Pioneers," he said, turning on my light.

Normally, I wouldn't care if Russ was freaked out because the kinds of things he usually freaked out about were math problems and other stuff that didn't matter.

But if he was concerned about the team, I needed to pay attention.

"What do you mean?" I asked, sitting up in bed and rubbing my eyes.

"We're playing really well together, right?"

"Definitely," I said, nodding.

"We're passing, shooting, and communicating better than ever."

"Yeah, thanks to solid teamwork. Why are you worried about that?"

"I'm not," he said, adjusting his glasses. "I'm worried that these twins are going to upset the balance of the team."

"Upset the . . . what?"

He shook his head. "Maybe I'm overthinking this, but I don't want a couple of brand-new guys to interfere with what's working for us."

"*Hmm*," I said quietly. He was right. We didn't need anyone to show up out of nowhere and mess with our system.

"Never mind. I'm probably just being paranoid," he said. "I'm going to bed."

After he left, I lay awake for a little while, thinking about the new twins.

What was the deal with them making the team without even trying out, anyway? When Coach Baxter took over, he didn't care who had been on the roster before, or that the guys and me had been playing together forever. We'd all had to prove ourselves at tryouts.

And those matching bozos were just going to walk on? It wasn't fair.

🏀   🏀   ⊕

In the morning, the twins were still on my mind as I got into the shower.

I didn't care that they were supposed to be big and athletic or that they had their own letterman jackets.

Okay, maybe I did care about that part. The point is, they should have been treated the same as the rest of us.

In the middle of thinking about it, I got a big blob of shampoo in my eye. It stung like crazy and I spent the rest of my shower too busy trying to prevent blindness to think about basketball or those stupid twins.

By the time I was dressed and ready for breakfast in the kitchen, my eye was still red and watery.

"Owen?" Mom said, looking worried. "Have you been crying?"

"No," I said, keeping the stinging eye closed. I told her about the shampoo and she helped me rinse it, but it still didn't feel much better.

By the time I sat down and started to dig into my waffle, Russ had made it to the kitchen.

I saw out of my one good eye that he was wearing the awesome Blazer hoodie Dad got him . . . with a checkered collared shirt underneath it. I'd told him a hundred times that he'd never look cool dressing like that.

And even worse? Instead of jeans or sweats, like the rest of the guys, he was wearing his brown cords. And they were so short, I could see his brown socks sticking out from the tops of his Nikes.

Oh, brother.

"Are you okay?" Russell asked when he sat down across from me and grabbed the syrup.

"I'm fine," I told him. "You wanna maybe switch that shirt for a regular one?"

"You mean a turtleneck?" he asked.

"No," I said with a sigh, wondering what was "normal" about a turtleneck.

"Are you sure you're okay? You look like you've been crying," he said, looking worried.

I shrugged and told him about the shampoo, then rubbed my eye again, which only made it worse. Mom told me to stop, but I couldn't help it.

After breakfast, Russ and I met Chris outside so we could walk to school together. I knew Chris would dribble his ball the whole way there, as usual. He'd seen some show on ESPN about a player who had at least one finger on his basketball at all times, so Chris had started carrying his everywhere he went. I had the feeling he slept with it.

I was all about basketball, but that was overkill.

"Nice Blazer win last night," I said.

Chris asked, "Are you joking?"

"No. Why?"

"You winked when you said it."

"He's not winking," Russ explained. "He has shampoo in his eye."

"Why?"

"Why do you think?" I asked.

"No idea." He shrugged.

I rolled my eyes. Well, one of them, anyway. "It was an *accident!*" I snapped.

"Wow," Chris muttered. "Touchy."

We were quiet for a minute or so, and the only sound was his ball slapping against the sidewalk.

"We've got practice this afternoon," Chris finally said.

"With the new twins," I added.

"Do we know what positions they play?" Russ asked, as he adjusted his glasses.

"No idea," Chris said. "But I guess we'll find out."

"You know, I haven't even *seen* these guys yet. Are they in any of your classes?" I asked both of them.

"Not so far," Chris said.

Russ shook his head. "I doubt they'll pop up in any of my advanced classes."

He was probably right about that. Russ was the only mathlete I'd ever heard of, so the chances of the Minnesota twins being star players *and* geniuses were zero to none, as Dad would say.

When we got to school, Chris and I walked to our lockers, which were right next to each other, while Russ headed upstairs.

While I was pulling out my books, I kept checking the hallway for a sign of the new twins. It was like looking for Waldo in one of those books I used to love. And just like Waldo, I couldn't find them anywhere.

I went to English class, hoping at least one of the new guys would be in there so I could check him out, but I was surrounded by the same old kids who'd been there all year. And four of them asked me if I was either upset or had been crying.

As far as spotting the twins went, social studies was a dead end, and so was math.

Between each class, I looked at the swarm of students packing the hallway and searched for unfamiliar faces, but I came up empty (except for some girl who handed me a tissue, thinking I'd been crying).

That was getting old.

When I met up with the Pioneers at lunch, it turned out that both twins were in Nicky Chu's art class, and they both sat at Nate's table in English.

"They're in classes *together*?" I asked.

My less-than-stellar grades and the fact that Russ was a total brainiac meant that we were separated at school. Mom was happy about that because she didn't think it was "healthy" for us to be together 24-7.

"I guess." Nate shrugged. "And they're dressed the same again."

"The letterman jackets?" I asked. "Kind of a show-off move, huh?"

"I don't know," Paul said, spraying cracker crumbs all over the table as he spoke. "If I had a letterman jacket, I'd wear it all the time."

So would I, but I didn't want to admit it.

"It's not just the jackets, anyway," Nate said. "They've got the same shoes, jeans, and everything. They even have the same haircut."

That was too weird for me. I never would have dressed like Russ, and not just because he had no style. I liked having my own look.

Once I knew that the twins were dressed the same again, I figured they'd be twice as easy to spot in the cafeteria, but I couldn't see them anywhere.

Those kids were like freakin' ghosts.

I made it through my afternoon classes and raced down to the locker room as soon as the final bell rang. I was excited about practice because any time on the court was a good time, but at least half of my speed was about finally seeing our new team members.

All my practice gear was crammed into my bag, which slammed into my leg every time I took a step. I even nailed a sixth grader in the stomach when I rounded the final corner way too fast.

"Are you okay?" I asked as I gasped for breath.

He nodded, and I took off again, taking the stairs down to the locker room two at a time.

"Hey, O," Russ said as he finished pulling up his socks.

"Hey," I said, but barely looked at him. I saw Nicky Chu, Nate, Paul, and four other guys from the team getting ready, but no new guys. "Have you seen them yet?"

"Who?" my brother asked.

"The *twins*."

"No," he said. "Maybe they're already out there."

I changed into my shorts and shirt as fast as I could and told Russ I'd catch him in the gym.

It barely took half a second for me to spot the Minnesota twins. They were supertall, with blond hair combed to one side and glued in place with some kind of hair goo.

Even though I knew what to expect, it was still weird to see two people who really did look exactly the same.

And I mean *exactly*.

They were wearing matching Timberwolves T-shirts, which would have to change, now that they were in Blazer territory. And along with their dark-blue shorts and blue Adidas, they both wore black rubber watches or bracelets on their wrists. Even the swooshes on their stinkin' Nike socks lined up with each other.

They were taking turns practicing shots and my stomach got all twisted.

The first twin make a textbook layup, then passed the ball to his brother. Twin number two made the exact same move, just as smoothly, and I felt like I was watching an instant replay instead of two totally different (but exactly the same) kids.

It almost made me dizzy.

Russ had been right to be worried.

These guys were definitely going to throw off the team's balance.

"When Chris said identical, he meant it," Russ whispered.

I'd been so focused, I hadn't even heard him sneak up behind me.

"No doubt," I said, nodding.

The twins didn't say anything or even look at each other, but one caught a pass there's no way he saw coming.

Like magic.

"How did he do that?" Russ whispered.

"I have no idea," I said.

And how did they manage to hit every single basket, too?

They were freaks of nature.

When I got tired of watching total perfection, I decided to introduce myself.

"Come on," I told Russ, and led the way across the court.

The twins had each made another basket by the time we got to them.

"Hey," I said.

They both stopped and turned to face me. Their faces were blank, like they hadn't decided how to feel about me yet.

Right back at you, I thought.

"Hey," they said at the exact same time. It was like surround-sound TV. No joke.

"Uh, I'm Owen, and this is my brother, Russ."

They both looked us over. "I'm Mitch, and he's Marcus," one finally said.

"They call us M&M," the other added.

"Peanut or chocolate?" I asked, chuckling.

They didn't even crack a smile.

"Or the Twofer," Marcus added, then explained, "We're twins."

Like they needed to explain *that*.

"So are we," Russell piped up. "Fraternal twins, I mean."

"Yup," I said, smiling at both of them.

"Did you just wink at me?" Mitch asked, looking surprised.

"What? No."

"He had trouble in the shower this morning," my brother explained.

Trouble in the shower? *Come on, Russ.*

"I got some shampoo in my eye, okay?" I muttered.

"*Okay*," Mitch said, giving his twin a look like I was speaking another language.

"So, what do you guys play?" I asked. "I mean, what positions?"

"Forward," Marcus said, starting to dribble the ball slowly.

"Both of you?"

"Uh, *yeah*," Mitch said, bouncing his own ball as they shared another look.

"And you're from Minnesota?"

"Twin Cities," they said together and nodded.

"Very funny," I snorted, and they shared another look.

"Minneapolis and Saint Paul," Russ said quietly. "They're called the Twin Cities, O."

The conversation wasn't going quite the way I'd planned, and thanks to their moving around while they dribbled, I'd already mixed up which twin was which.

Was Marcus on the right?

"So," I said, pointing to their shirts, "you guys like the Timberwolves, huh?"

"Wolves," one of them said.

"Yeah," the other one said. "Just the Wolves."

I tried again. "I guess you'll be swapping those out for Blazer gear pretty soon."

"Yeah, right," one said.

"Why bother? The Pioneers are already wearing Wolves colors," the other one said, laughing.

"No, they're—" I started to say, but he was right. Blue and white, all the way.

Why didn't we wear red, black, and white like our NBA team?

"So are you guys—" I began to ask, but the twins cut me off.

"We should be warming up," they said, in stereo again.

They gave each other another one of their stupid looks.

I didn't want them to know it bugged me. "Cool," I said with a nod.

Russ and I watched them walk away.

"I don't like this," he said quietly.

"Neither do I."

Perfect Square

I should have felt better about the Matthews twins once I'd met them and all the mystery was gone.

But the reality that was left where the mystery used to be was worse.

It was strange to see two people look so alike, and after admiring their precisely parted hair, I couldn't help reaching up to touch the uncontrollable mop on the top of my own head.

I glanced at Owen, who is stocky and several inches shorter than I am. He always describes us as looking like a pencil and an eraser.

What if we had been born identical?

I glanced back at M&M, still amazed by how similar they were.

But even more interesting than their appearance was that they were confident, expert players with a closer connection than any brothers or sisters I'd ever seen.

They were *in tune* with each other.

And wouldn't Coach Baxter rather have two players who were in tune with each other out on the court than two who weren't?

I looked at Owen again. Never mind the tune. We weren't even listening to the same kind of music.

Why would Coach give us game time instead of the Matthews twins?

The answer was simple: he wouldn't.

I felt a shiver scurry up my spine.

Basketball had become very important to me, very quickly, and I'd never thought about losing it all so easily.

What if there wasn't room for me on the team anymore?

I was enjoying my role as the school's athlete so much, I wasn't sure how I would handle going back to being *just* the brains.

I could feel the stress building up inside me, so I started thinking about the periodic table, which usually calmed me down.

Elements that begin with "A": actinium, aluminum, americium . . .

"Okay, Pioneers," Coach Baxter shouted, then blew his whistle to call us to center court.

"Here we go," Owen muttered.

I followed the rest of the guys over to the huddle, already missing them. They'd become my friends as well as my teammates.

I shook my head, knowing I was being unreasonable. After all, the Matthews twins hadn't replaced me.

Yet.

"I want you to meet your new teammates, Mitch and Marcus." Coach pointed to each of the brothers. Judging by the looks on their faces, he hadn't matched the right names with the faces. "They're new transfers, from Saint Paul, Minnesota."

The rest of the Pioneers nodded but didn't say anything.

"So," Coach continued, "I know there's been some grumbling about tryouts, but I don't want to punish these guys because they moved here midseason."

"I do," Owen whispered.

"I think that once you see these boys play, you'll agree that we're lucky to have them." He smiled at our new teammates. "Very lucky."

And that was the end of the discussion.

I don't know what I was expecting. I should have realized that basketball, unlike Masters of the Mind, was not a democracy. What Coach said, went.

As I ran laps around the gym for our warm-up, which was the most grueling part of my week, I watched Mitch and Marcus run together. Their strides perfectly mirrored one another, their elbows moved in unison, and their chests rose and fell in time when they inhaled and exhaled.

It was like they were one person, split into two bodies.

Watching them, I was embarrassed by my jerky legs and flailing arms. They looked natural, like they were born to run while I wasn't even sure I was born to *walk*.

When Owen lapped me for the second time, I paid attention to how steady his pace was, and how he kept his head high.

For the first time I could remember, I wished that my brother and I were more alike.

And I kept wishing for that as the practice went on.

Coach Baxter had us line up for all the usual drills, but seeing the Matthews twins in action was like watching an instructional video.

Basically, they were the "dos" while I was a "don't."

✕   ÷   ✚

"Nice play," Nicky Chu shouted during the scrimmage at the end of practice. M&M had just dazzled all of us with an unbelievable joint effort to score yet another basket.

"Now *that* was a no-look pass," Paul said, shaking his head. "How'd they do it?"

That was what I wanted to know.

Owen and I worked well together on the court, but we couldn't coordinate moves like the new twins even if our lives depended on it.

Thankfully, they didn't.

"Shoot, Russ!" Nate shouted the next time I had the ball.

I hesitated as one M came toward me. He was the tallest player I'd ever gone up against, and he had at least three inches on me. Of course, that meant they both did, so I should have been expecting the other reaching arm that came from behind me and snatched the ball.

But I wasn't.

"Like candy from a baby," one of them said as he dribbled away from me.

I wished I could tell them apart, so I'd know which one was the jerk.

Then again, maybe they both were.

"Don't let them get to you, Russ," Owen said as he ran past me.

At that precise moment, one of them threw the ball toward the basket and the other came flying through the air to *dunk* it.

I'd only seen an "alley-oop" on TV, completed by professionals.

Don't let them get to me? It was a bit late for that.

By the time practice was over, the entire Pioneer roster (except for my brother and me) was awestruck by the new guys.

"I can't believe how good they are," Chris whispered as we walked off the court. "No one's going to be able to stop us this year."

Owen frowned. "I thought we were doing pretty awesome without them."

"Yeah, I know." He nodded. "But this is a whole new level, man. A whole new game."

Judging by the expression on my brother's face, I knew he felt the same way I did.

We liked the game the way it used to be.

✖ ➗ ➕

When we sat down at the dinner table that night, Mom asked how practice had gone.

"We got a couple of new guys on the team," Owen told her. "Twins, from Minnesota."

"Ah, the Minnesota Twins," Dad said, chuckling.

Mom didn't look like she knew about the baseball team either. I had the feeling that, like a lot of other sports facts, we might be the only people alive who didn't.

"They're good," I said.

"As good as you two?" Dad asked, doubtfully.

"Better," I told him.

"Whoa! Speak for yourself," Owen said.

"I meant as a pair, they're better than we are." It was the truth, and sometimes the truth hurt. In fact, sometimes it stung like you were being attacked by a swarm of Asian hornets. And I use them as an example because their stings contain more of the pain-causing chemical acetylcholine than any other insect. *That's* how much it stung to know how good the Matthews twins were.

"Better than us? You really think so?" Owen asked.

"Did you watch the drills? They were perfectly synchronized."

"Yeah, well the rest of the Pioneers can be synchronized."

"Sure," I told him. "When they do the hokey pokey."

"Russ," Owen said, his expression very serious. "None of us do the hokey pokey."

I rolled my eyes. "I was just making a point."

"Well, geez, don't make that one."

"Okay, drills aside, did you watch the scrimmage?"

"I was playing, Russ. So yeah, I was watching."

"Then maybe you noticed that they were like . . . a machine?"

"We're still talking about a pair of twelve-year-old boys, right?" Mom asked.

"Yes," I said, attempting to scoop several unwilling peas onto my fork.

"Because right now they're sounding like something out of a Spielberg movie."

"*Twinvaders of the Third Kind*," Dad said, smiling.

"That fits," Owen said, then started speaking in a ghoulish voice. "They came out of the darkness to take over the team."

"Minnesota is hardly the darkness," Mom said, rolling her eyes. "In case you've forgotten, I grew up in Wisconsin."

Owen looked completely lost.

"It's the state next door," I whispered.

"Oh," he said, like the country had been modified and he hadn't seen the new map yet.

"Anyway," I said, trying to bring the conversation back to the original topic. "Maybe 'machine' is the wrong word. They were more like . . ." I tried to think of how to describe the way they moved around the court as if they were attached with an invisible rope, always the right distance apart, each of them anticipating what the other was going to do. And then it hit me. "They were like Kevin Maple and Adam Donaldson."

"You've lost me," Mom said, shaking her head.

"Blazers," Dad explained, then turned to me. "How so, Russ?"

"It's hard to explain. They just seemed to be in tune with each other. They didn't have to say anything, or make eye contact or—"

"They were mind-reading Twinvaders from outer space," Owen said, in that same creepy voice.

"I didn't say they were telepathic, Owen," I reminded him, feeling irritated. "They just seem to have . . . an understanding."

"Well," Dad said, reaching for another piece of chicken. "That would make sense, wouldn't it? Maple and Donaldson played together for three solid years in college. These Matthews twins have probably been playing together all their lives."

That was a very good point.

I picked up my chicken wing and started gnawing on the pointy tip while I thought about what Dad had said.

Owen and I had been playing together for only four *weeks*. In that short amount of time, we couldn't expect to have created the kind of on-court connection that the Matthews twins shared.

And while Owen and I might not have had that connection yet, we could work on building it.

I started right there at the table with my chicken dinner. I mirrored my brother, lifting my fork at the same time and speed as he did. I ate my vegetables in the same order and drank my milk with the same annoyingly small sips that he did.

When Mom brought out bowls of ice cream, instead of eating it like a normal person, I stirred it until it had the texture of a milk shake, just like Owen did.

"Will you cut it out?" he asked.

"What?" I asked.

"Stop copying me."

"I'm not copying you," I told him. "I'm getting in tune with you. I'm hoping that it will help our game."

"That's crazy," Owen said, rolling his eyes and turning his attention to his ice-cream soup.

Maybe it was.

I scooped a drippy spoonful into my mouth and wished I'd left it alone.

$$\times \quad \div \quad +$$

When I arrived in my science class a few minutes early the next morning, I set up my work station just the way I liked it. We were in the middle of a geology section, and even though I preferred to study physics and chemistry, I was enjoying it.

I had just opened my textbook to reread the chapters I'd studied the night before when two long shadows spread across my page.

I glanced up and saw Mitch and Marcus standing over me, blocking the light from the windows. They were wearing matching University of Minnesota baseball hats and the letterman jackets I was beginning to think they never took off.

"Hey, Owen," one of them said.

"Actually, I'm Russell," I told him.

They couldn't tell *us* apart?

"Oh, sure," he said, nodding. "Hey, Russell."

"Hey," I replied, wondering what on earth they were doing in Mrs. Lansdowne's lab. "Are you looking for a classroom? I know the layout of the school is a bit strange, but—"

"This *is* our classroom," one of them said.

"You're taking accelerated science?" I asked doubtfully.

"Yes," they said at the same time.

"Both of . . . you're *both* registered for accelerated science?"

They nodded again. "And advanced math," they said together.

This can't be happening.

I'd already seen how amazing they were on the court, and now they were going to excel in academics, too?

I glanced from one identical face to the other, feeling my body fill with dread.

"What are we studying?" one of them asked.

"Geology," I told them as I flipped open the cover of my textbook to show them. "We've been talking about the layers of the earth and—"

"Our dad is a geologist," they said at the exact same time.

"Oh," I said quietly.

"He specializes in plate tectonics," one continued.

What I knew about plate tectonics couldn't fill one of the glass beakers on the shelf in front of me.

"That's interesting," I said glumly.

I could already imagine them at the top of the class, smiling down at me with identical dimples.

It was one thing to be outplayed on the basketball court, but in the lab, too?

That, as Owen would say, was pushing it.

Jump Ball

Ever since the first practice, where they had totally dominated the court, I'd been worried that the Twinvaders were going to take over the Pioneers in two or three quick moves.

They were so good, it was ridiculous!

And the other guys thought so, too.

I noticed that Nate had started to copy them, like wearing a black rubber bracelet on his wrist. And Paul had asked them eight hundred questions about Minnesota, as if he actually cared how cold it got there or how big the mosquitoes were.

The guys were acting like Mitch and Marcus were movie stars or something, and it was really starting to bug me. After all, we'd grown up together and always been equals. No one on the team had been special, no matter how well they played. And now these two strangers were being treated like they'd invented the freakin' game.

Even worse, they acted like they deserved to have the rest of us Pioneers as *fans*!

I mean, *come on*.

I tried to talk to Chris about it at our lockers one morning.

"It must be nice to go from zeros to heroes in less than a week, huh?" I asked as I pulled out my math book.

"What?" Chris asked, looking confused.

"The new twins."

"Zeros to heroes?"

"Yeah, they came out of nowhere and now they're worshiped by everybody."

Chris shook his head. "I don't think they were zeros in Minnesota, O. Their team went to state last year."

I rolled my eyes. "You know what I mean."

"Not really," he said. "Nobody's worshiping them. I think everybody's just excited that two more awesome players joined the team."

"Without trying out," I reminded him.

"Yeah," he said, shrugging. "But like Coach said, it's not their fault they transferred midseason."

Frustrated because my best friend had been brainwashed, I told Chris I'd catch him later.

Just like every other day at lunchtime, the Pioneers made sure that there was enough room at our table for the Twinvaders.

And just like every other day so far, they hadn't shown up.

"Do you think they go home to eat?" Nate asked.

"No idea," I told him. And who cared, anyway?

"You invited them to sit with us, right?" Paul asked Nicky Chu.

"Yeah, during art class."

I rolled my eyes as I bit into my tuna and sprout sandwich. They probably thought they were too good to eat with us.

Why couldn't anyone else see that they were jerks?

By the time our next game rolled around, I was feeling kind of nervous. It would be the first game for the Matthews twins, and I didn't know what to expect.

I concentrated even less in my classes than usual, and when I got nailed in the head by a piece of beef jerky at lunch, I barely even noticed.

"Think Coach will start them?" Nate asked the table.

"M&M?" Paul asked. "Totally."

"Seriously?" I practically choked.

"Wouldn't you?" Nicky Chu asked. "I mean, if you had that kind of a combo ready to go, wouldn't you want to give them as many minutes as you could?"

I took another big bite of my tuna sandwich so I wouldn't have to answer.

"Where's Russ?" Chris asked a couple of minutes later.

"Hanging out with his Masters team, I guess." I glanced at their table and saw that he'd laid out his apple, cookies, and drink and was pointing in turn at each of them. He seemed to be using them to explain . . . well, *something*.

"You think he'll get cut?" Nate asked.

It took me a second to realize that he was talking about basketball.

"From the team?" I asked, surprised.

"Well, yeah." Paul shrugged. "We already had a full roster."

Nate nodded. "And if we're two guys over—"

"Did Coach say he'd be cutting?" I practically choked.

"No, but—"

"Then don't even bring it up!"

As long as Coach didn't have plans to trim the team, it was all just talk and Russ was safe.

I'd just have to hope it stayed that way.

I made it to the locker room right after the last bell. Nicky Chu and Russ were already in there, getting dressed for the game.

"You guys ready?" I asked, pulling my jersey out of my bag. Mom had ironed it the night before, but after a day of being jammed in my locker, it was a wrinkled mess.

"Always," Nicky Chu said, at the same time Russ mumbled, "I hope so."

He *hoped* so?

"What's wrong?" I asked my brother.

"Nothing," he said. "I mean, I'm just wondering how things are going to play out today."

I was worried about the new guys taking over the Pioneers and winning over the fans, too, but I knew it was my job to keep it together, no matter how I was feeling inside.

"We're going to go out there and score a ton of baskets. That's how it's going to play out."

The words felt good coming out of my mouth.

"That's what I like to hear," a voice said from behind me.

I turned to see both twins dressed in their Pioneer uniforms. Coach had given out all the numbered jerseys at the beginning of the season, so Mitch and Marcus were stuck with blank ones until the new order came in. It kind of stunk, because I'd been counting on the numbers to figure out which of them was which.

"Yeah." I nodded. "And believe me, beating West Slope won't be a problem." I liked how tough that sounded.

"They're a smaller school," Russ explained, totally taking the toughness out of it.

"We used to play some—" one of the twins began.

"Huge schools," the other finished for him.

"Massive," they said in unison.

"Yeah, well, we've got some pretty massive schools here, too," I told them.

"Sure, you do." They gave each other another one of those weird looks, like they were the only ones who understood anything.

That was really starting to tick me off.

But I didn't have time to worry about it because I could hear Coach blowing his whistle out in the gym.

"Let's roll!" I said, heading for the hardwood.

When I jogged over to Coach and the rest of the guys, I waved to some of the fans who cheered for me.

At the far basket, I could see the West Slope team taking shots. I'd always heard they played hard to prove they were better than their purple and orange uniforms, which had to be the ugliest in the league. Judging by their warm-up, the rumors were true.

But they'd never be warm enough for the Pioneers.

Our winning streak was going to stay red hot.

"I want to mix things up a little today," Coach said, once we were all in the huddle.

Uh-oh.

I took a deep breath, knowing that when Coach mixed things up, it was usually bad news.

"I'm going to have Nicky and Chris start as guards, but I want the Matthews boys as forwards. Paul, you stick to center."

Wait. What?

The only regular starters who'd be on the bench at tip-off were *Russ and me*?

I tried to shoot my brother a look, the way the Twinvaders did, but he was too busy watching Coach to notice.

Mitch and Marcus didn't even ask who would be playing small forward and who would be power forward, which could only mean one thing. Both of them could play both positions.

The situation was even worse than I thought.

Especially when they jumped up in the air and bumped their chests together.

I tried to imagine Russ and me pulling a move like that, but all I could picture was Russ wiping out.

Once Coach let us break huddle, I went straight to the basket to take a few practice shots of my own. When he put me in, I was going to have to seriously shine.

And I did during the warm-up.

I made a couple of layups, nice and easy, trying to concentrate on the good stuff. Like the sound of everybody's shoes squeaking against the floor, and hearing how excited my teammates were about the game.

I took a deep breath.

I loved basketball and I wasn't going to let a short ride on the bench change that.

After a couple of minutes of dribbling and shooting, I noticed that the Matthews brothers were dribbling, too. But they were bouncing the balls under their legs and around their backs, like they were the freakin' Harlem Globetrotters.

I mean, *come on*.

Before I could even try to copy some of their moves, the ref blew his whistle. I took another deep breath and started walking toward the bench.

When I passed my new teammates, they high-fived each other, which was something me and my uncoordinated brother could never do, and shouted, "Twin it to win it!"

I looked at Russ, who shook his head.

As the players lined up for the tip-off, the two of us sat together, our eyes glued to our teammates.

When the ref tossed the ball, Paul easily tapped it over to a Twinvader, and I could see why Coach wanted three big guys up there. The twin passed to his brother, over the heads and waving hands of the West Slope players.

I watched Mitch and Marcus weave through the other players, taking huge strides the shorter kids needed two or three steps to match.

One of the twins spun around and whipped a bounce pass to his brother, who dribbled a couple of times, then fired the ball back with another no-look pass, perfectly on target.

The first twin went for the basket and scored the first two points of the game, like it was nothing.

As I watched them play, I saw how they moved together and how each brother always seemed to know exactly where the other one was on the court. I didn't think they could read each other's minds, like my sci-fi-loving brother did, but he was right about them being "in tune" with each other.

Too bad I didn't like the song.

I watched one of the twins throw the ball toward the basket, and I knew we were in for *another* alley-oop. The second one jumped into the air at just the right moment and scored. It was like they'd planned out the whole game six months ago and practiced each move, over and over again, so they'd look like pros.

It was spooky.

But even I had to admit it was awesome. Ugh.

"You're up, Evans," Coach said, near the end of the first quarter.

I looked at Russ, who shrugged.

"That was Evans, plural. Both of you get out there," Coach said.

He didn't have to tell me twice. (Well, actually, I guess he did.)

I can't even describe how happy I was to be bumping Mitch and Marcus back to the bench, even if it was only for a few minutes.

They'd done a ton of damage while they'd been playing, racking up seventeen points between them. Sure, that damage had also put us in the lead.

But still.

I ran toward the twins, shouting, "Subbing for Matthews" because I wasn't totally sure which one I was replacing.

I felt like a hero coming home, even though the bench was only a few feet away from the game. I could almost hear the crowd breathe a sigh of relief as they watched me jog across the hardwood.

The Matthews boys were good, but they were still strangers.

Everybody knew they could count on the Evans twins.

Russ was right beside me, and it felt awesome, knowing that my brother and me were about to be back in business.

I heard a girl scream, "Let's see that Russell Hustle!"

I'd gotten used to his trademark cheer, but Russ hadn't. His face turned bright red.

Then he tripped over his shoelaces.

"Double knots," I muttered for about the ten thousandth time since he'd started playing.

So much for looking like returning superstars.

Russ quickly retied his laces and I helped him back to his feet.

"Are we ready?" the ref asked, and I could tell he wasn't happy about the delay.

"For sure," I told him, high-fiving Nate and Paul, then sizing up the sea of purple and orange in front of me.

The ref blew his whistle, and it was go time!

It felt really good to be back in the game, and the second

I got the ball, I took off for the net. But I got blocked so I passed to Nate, who was totally ready for it.

Take that, Twinvaders!

Teamwork had nothing to do with DNA.

Nate took a shot, but the ball bounced off the rim.

"Good try," I said, as we ran back down the court. "We'll get another chance."

And we did. Right after West Slope scored, we were heading back toward their net to answer their two points with two of our own.

Paul passed me the ball, then I swerved around the guy guarding me and dribbled around another.

I was in the zone, like we were filming a Nike commercial or something.

I thought about the new guys and their smooth, perfect moves. I thought about those alley-oops and no-look passes.

And that gave me an idea.

The rest of the Pioneers and I were "in tune," too, weren't we? We had plenty of practices and games under our belts.

And the winning streak was ours. *We* were the ones who'd earned it.

I couldn't wait for the crowd to see exactly how good we were, so I dribbled a second longer, then whipped the ball over to Russ. It was my first ever no-look pass, and I waited for the cheering to start.

But I heard something else, instead.

"*Oof!*"

I turned to see the ball bounce out of bounds while Russ rubbed his head and bent to pick up his glasses.

Oops.

No one was cheering. In fact, they were all just staring at me.

"What was that?" Paul demanded.

"A no-look pass?" I said, wincing. "Sorry, Russ."

"Why no-look?" my brother asked, then shook his head, probably realizing he sounded like Tarzan. "I mean, why didn't you look?"

Because I thought it would be cool probably wasn't the best answer.

I glanced at the bench and saw the brothers shaking their heads while Coach Baxter's mouth hung open.

I looked back at Russ. "I thought you'd know it was coming."

"How?"

Duh. He was the one who brought up all the "in tune" stuff, not me.

"Maybe give him a little heads-up next time," Nate muttered. "Geez, Owen."

"Are you okay to play?" the ref asked.

Russ nodded. "I'm fine."

West Slope had the ball, and the first thing they did after the whistle was score.

From that moment on, it seemed like every move I made

was the wrong one. My passes were crummy, my shots were lame, and my dribbling was like . . . Russ's.

"I'm open!" I shouted, when he had the ball.

The rest of the Pioneers could tell I was having a rough game, but Russ didn't let that stop him. He passed it way too high, and when I jumped up to get it, I bumped into a West Slope player and landed hard on my tailbone.

Just what I needed.

I got back on my feet, knowing I had to get my head away from the Twinvaders and back in the game.

But it was tough.

Even when we made a good play—like when Paul stole the ball and passed to Nate, who was in the perfect position to score . . . and did—it just wasn't the same as watching the Matthews twins play. Our moves didn't have their wow factor.

And I wanted the wow. Big-time.

Alternate Angles

If the first game with the Matthews twins wasn't enough of an eye-opener, my math class had me bug-eyed.

Mr. Hollis was in the middle of a fairly complicated word problem involving multiple cars, cities, and driving distances. While I took notes, I glanced over at Nitu, who was a bona-fide math whiz, and smiled when I saw that her calculations almost filled an entire page in her notebook.

Nitu was always at least two steps ahead of me when it came to numbers, and that was saying something.

I turned back to my page and continued taking notes. All I heard around me were the sounds of pencils scratching paper and the backs of hands brushing eraser bits off of desktops.

It was like music to my ears.

I wrote down all the important details in my own special form of shorthand (when Owen saw it for the first time, he thought I'd created an alien language), and I had a pretty good idea of how to solve the problem.

I was practically humming to myself.

"Mr. Hollis?" one M said, interrupting the moment.

"Please raise your hand if you have a question," the teacher requested. He was kind of a stickler for classroom rules, which was one of my favorite things about him.

After all, what kind of a world would it be without rules?

The twin sighed and lifted one hand as if it was the most ridiculous thing in the world to do.

As if Mr. Hollis had asked him to scale Mt. Everest with no boots.

That attitude wasn't going to get him very far in this class, and there was a small part of me that felt excited, knowing that things were about to turn around for at least one of the Matthews twins.

"Yes?" Mr. Hollis said, holding his chalk a couple of inches from the board.

"Your answer will be wrong."

My mouth dropped open almost as fast as Nitu's did.

"I beg your pardon?" Mr. Hollis said, eyebrows raised in surprise. He probably hadn't been on the receiving end of the word "wrong" in years.

I turned in my seat, wondering what on earth the twin was going to say next.

Naturally, I wasn't sure which one had spoken.

"Arizona doesn't—" one of the boys said.

"Change their clocks," the other finished.

They sounded like they'd been practicing the sentence for years, just like everything else I'd seen or heard from them.

How did they both know what to say? I hadn't heard them whispering, and I could see from my desk that their notebook pages were blank.

Completely blank.

"So," the first twin continued, "if you don't take into account the fact that Oregon adjusts for daylight savings while Arizona stays on mountain time and doesn't roll back their clocks in November, your train's arrival time in Phoenix is going to be off by an hour."

I gulped.

Daylight savings?

No one had said anything about daylight savings.

I looked at the scribbles on my page.

Why hadn't *I* thought about daylight savings?

Mr. Hollis cleared his throat, but before he could speak, the second twin said, "Unless we say that the train trip is happening sometime after next March, when our clocks spring forward and line up with Arizona's again."

Mr. Hollis frowned.

The other twin nodded. "That would solve it."

"Mr. Hollis?" his brother asked. "Should we say the train trip is—"

"Happening next spring?" his twin finished for him.

"Uh . . . yes," the teacher said. It was the first time I'd ever seen him at a loss for words.

And I didn't have much to say either.

On the way out of class, Nitu shook her head. "That was interesting."

"Yes, it was," I agreed. Interesting *and* annoying.

"I can't believe they thought about something so random. Daylight savings never would have crossed my mind. I mean, I just stick to what's on the page."

"So does Mr. Hollis, obviously."

She shrugged. "It was kind of cool."

That was the last thing I needed to hear.

"Especially when they finished each other's sentences," she continued. "I'm telling you, there's something to that twin telepathy."

× ÷ +

The more I thought about it, the more it bothered me that Mitch and Marcus were so closely connected. They could anticipate each other's moves on the basketball court, they shared the same way of thinking through problems, and they even finished each other's sentences.

I wanted that bond with Owen.

At dinner that night, I thought back to my attempt at trying to get in tune with him through eating. Yes, I had failed, but many experiments failed the first time. If no one was willing to try again, we wouldn't have cars, televisions, or even lightbulbs.

Yes, I would try again.

My hope was that if we could develop the same kind of bond as M&M shared, we could be as strong as they were on the court. An academic bond with Owen was out of the question, obviously.

So, I laid my napkin on my lap at the same time that Owen did, then lifted my glass of milk, matching him perfectly, sip for sip.

With relief, I noted that mirroring his movements was a bit easier the second time around.

When he lifted his fork, I lifted mine.

I knew it was a very simple idea, but some of the best ideas in the world were simple. I could practically feel the bond between us growing stronger.

He pierced a piece of broccoli and I did the same, then started to lift it toward my mouth. But instead of Owen doing the same thing, he moved the fork to spear a piece of steak. I hesitated, but followed his lead.

Then he scooped up some mashed potatoes.

When I saw that he was going to shovel those different

foods with those different tastes and textures into his mouth *at the same time*, I gagged.

"Russell?" Mom asked. "Are you okay?"

"I'm fine," I told her, though I was far from it.

I didn't even like my foods to touch on my plate, let alone in my mouth!

I removed the steak from my fork and sighed.

Apparently, getting in sync with Owen was going to happen somewhere other than at the dinner table.

But I wasn't giving up yet.

× ÷ +

My next attempt to get closer to my brother was at the following Pioneers practice, where we ran laps to warm up. In no time at all, my lungs burned and my legs felt like they weighed at least a ton. Each.

But I was on a mission, so I pushed myself to run faster than ever before. And I did. But I was still lapped by the perfectly synchronized Matthews twins, which was all the encouragement I needed to push even harder.

By the time I caught up with Owen and Chris, I was sticky with sweat and gasping for breath.

"Whoa, Russ!" Owen said. "What's going on?"

"Nothing," I told him, having to split the word up over two gasps to get it out of my mouth. "Just warming up."

"Don't kill yourself," Chris said. "We'll have a whole practice to do that."

"I know," I said, and choked.

We ran in silence, aside from my panting, for about twenty seconds. It felt like an hour and a half.

"Are you guys watching the game tonight?" Chris asked.

"Definitely," Owen told him. "Right, Russ?"

"Yeah," I said, and gasped.

"What do you think about Will Sanders?" Chris asked, looking to me for an answer.

I was supposed to keep up with their insane pace, breathe, *and* carry on a conversation?

Really?

I glanced at Mitch and Marcus, who were chatting away like they were on a stroll instead of a death sprint. The soles of their Adidas hit the floor at the exact same time, every time, and it didn't even look as if they were trying.

Which meant I had to try harder.

"He's good," I grunted at Chris, even though I'd forgotten what player he was asking about.

"Blow out the air every couple of steps," Owen suggested. "Don't keep sucking more in."

And risk my lungs deflating completely? "I'm okay," I croaked.

"No, you aren't. Trust me, it'll help," Owen insisted.

But breathing wasn't going to help me. Nothing was.

With each step I lost a bit of speed, until I was trailing them by a couple of feet, then half a lap.

Keeping up just wasn't in the cards.

When Coach Baxter finally blew the whistle to stop the torture, I'd never been more grateful for anything in my life. I walked in circles for a few seconds, hands on my waist while I caught my breath. I tried to ignore the fact that none of the other guys were even slightly winded.

"Winning streak or not, we still need to work on some basics," Coach said. "Starting with free throws."

My specialty! I couldn't help smiling.

Coach split us up into two groups, and I was assigned to the far net with Nicky Chu, Paul, and a handful of the other guys, including M&M.

Terrific.

We lined up to take turns shooting, and I somehow ended up sandwiched between the twins.

"My brother and I want to stand together," the one behind me said.

"Oh, uh . . . sure," I told him, moving aside.

They couldn't be two feet away from each other?

The twins waited their turn, exchanging smiles and nods I couldn't even begin to understand. It was like speaking without words. Sign language without the signs.

Telepathy.

"What are they doing?" Nicky Chu whispered.

I shook my head instead of answering, trying to imagine doing the same thing with Owen and not succeeding.

Coach blew his whistle and the first twin dribbled to the free throw line and held the ball under one arm while he shook the other to loosen it up, then crouched and straightened a couple of times. When I thought he was ready, he crouched and straightened again.

Was it basketball or ballet class?

He finally took the shot, which soared through the air in a perfect arc and dropped right through the net with a silent but deadly *swish*.

"Sweet," Nicky Chu said quietly.

And I had to admit it *was* sweet. That is, until the second Matthews brother did the exact same thing, right down to shaking his hands loose and crouching.

"Amazing," Paul said. "They're *exactly* the same."

There was another silent *swish*, and the ball was passed to me.

I was a terrible dribbler, so I carried the ball to the free throw line. I liked taking shots when there was no one between me and the basket, and the silence made me feel calm. I had time to relax my shoulders and every other body part before throwing the ball.

I took a deep breath.

"Nuts!" Owen shouted from the other basket as I heard a ball bounce off the far rim.

I sighed, then bounced the ball twice, took a deep breath, adjusted my glasses, licked my lips, and rolled my shoulders. I bent my knees and jumped in the air as I threw the ball.

It bounced off the backboard with a satisfying *thwack* and dropped right through the net.

Whew.

"Nice shot," one of the twins said as I joined them at the back of the line.

"Thank you," I said, smiling.

"Your stance is kind of weird, though," the other one added.

"Yeah, crooked," the first one agreed.

"But it was still a decent shot," the other said.

"Yeah, and a basket is a basket, even if you look—"

"Weird scoring it," they said together.

What?

Between the back of the line and my next turn shooting, all I could think about was my "crooked" stance. Dad had told me it was fine when we practiced, and I *had* scored, so did it matter if I looked weird shooting?

Yes, it did.

Metalloids: boron, silicon, germanium . . .

The twins took their next shots, and both were perfect.

Arsenic, antimony, tellurium . . .

The ball was passed to me and I took a deep breath as I approached the line for my second turn.

All I could think about was my crooked body.

"Try pushing off the other foot," one of the Matthews brothers called out to me.

My shoulders tensed.

"And relax," the other one added.

As if I could.

I exhaled and threw the ball, which fell about three feet short of the basket.

"Now *that* was a brick," the two voices said in unison.

I made my way to the back of the line and missed the next four shots I attempted.

I stood in line, waiting for my next humiliation and focused my attention straight ahead.

As I stewed over M&M's successful efforts to psych me out, I realized that I'd discovered a new element to add to the periodic table.

It was incredibly toxic and it was going to take helium's place, with an atomic number of two.

Twinidium.

Picked Off

Our game against Dante Powers and the rest of the Hogarth Huskies was coming up fast.

I was feeling more nervous about it than I wanted to. It seemed like I'd been looking forward to going head-to-head against Dante forever, but that was back in the days of the old-school Pioneers. Back when I only sat on the bench because I needed to catch my breath.

I'd had a couple of dreams about the game, and more than a few daydreams during class.

In my head, I beat Dante every time. I outdribbled, out-passed, and outshot him. I beat his state record *and* got carried off the court on my teammates' shoulders.

If even *one* of those things happened on game day, I'd be stoked.

But we had to play the Willamette Warriors first.

On Wednesday afternoon, the Pioneers piled onto the bus for the trip to Willamette, ready to keep our winning streak alive.

The Twinvaders didn't sit with the rest of us at the middle or the back of the bus, but instead right behind the driver. One of them pulled a notebook out of his backpack, and they studied it together.

Russ told me they were math superstars, but even my brainiac brother saved his homework for, well, *home*.

"What's the Warriors' record?" Russ asked from the seat next to me.

"Five and three," I told him. "Not as good as ours."

"But close."

"Yeah," I admitted. "We're close."

We couldn't say the same about Hogarth, who hadn't lost a game yet.

I shook my head. I needed to stop thinking about Dante Powers and concentrate on the game that was only half an hour away instead.

"Is there anything I should know about them?" Russ asked.

I shrugged. "Just that we have to win if we want to keep our streak going."

"No special tips?"

"Not really," I said, confused. Special tips?

He was quiet for a minute and I started trying to get my game face on.

"Are you going to wear your watch when we play?"

"What?" I asked, totally confused.

"Are you going to—"

I rolled my eyes. "I heard the question, Russ."

"So, are you?"

"I never do."

He nodded. "Cool." Then Russ cleared his throat. "Did you bring your Nike socks?"

I turned toward him. What was his deal? "Duh, Russ. I always wear them on game days."

"Cool," he said again. "You know, I've seen some kids wearing sweatbands. On their wrists?"

"Is that a question?"

"No." He frowned. "Well, maybe. Do you think you'd ever wear those?"

"Ha! Not in this lifetime."

"But NBA players wear them," Russ reasoned.

"No, *some* NBA players wear them," I corrected. "Not the ones I like."

"Gotcha," he said, nodding again.

I felt like I was taking a test and it was making me edgy. And I definitely didn't need to feel edgy before a game.

"What's with the twenty questions?" I asked.

Russ looked surprised. "I've only asked a couple."

"Yeah, but you look like you're just getting started." Before he could say anything else, I told him, "I'd just like some quiet time for now. Is that cool?"

Russ nodded.

But a bus packed with basketball players wasn't the place for quiet time.

While I looked out the window and tried to picture myself sinking a three-pointer, or even making a couple of good layups, the rest of the team cranked up the volume.

"How many points are we going to win by?" Chris yelled from the backseat.

"Thirty!" Nicky Chu shouted back.

"That would be sweet, but I'm betting more like fourteen," Paul said.

They went around the whole bus and every guy answered.

"What about you, Owen?" Nate asked.

"I don't know. Maybe eight?" I said.

"Russ?"

"I think eight, too," he said.

"You do?" I asked him, and he just shrugged and smiled.

When it was the Twinvaders' turn, they sounded like robots as they said at the exact same time, "We don't predict outcomes."

"How do they do that?" I muttered.

"I have no idea," Russ said with a sigh.

"Does anyone have an eraser?" one of the brothers asked the rest of us.

"Not in my gear bag," I muttered to Russ. "I mean, *come on*."

"I do," Russ said, reaching for one of the eight thousand zippers on his backpack.

"Cool," Mitch or Marcus said when Russ passed it forward. Then he actually *smiled* and kind of shrugged as he explained, "Miscalculation."

"*Minor* miscalculation," his twin corrected, loud enough for the whole bus to hear. Like anybody cared. "*Minor.*"

"Right," the one with the eraser said, his cheeks turning red. He nodded to Russ. "Thanks."

"No problem," Russ said, nodding back. After a second or two, he said, "I wonder what they're working on."

"A plan to take over the universe, I bet."

"You know, it's interesting. In math class the other day—"

"Hold up, Russ. I'm only telling you this to help you out, but unless somebody pukes, gets sent to the principal's office, or both, you should never start an *interesting* story with, 'in math class.'"

"Right, but—"

"Are you sure this story is going to be interesting?"

"Maybe not to you," Russ admitted.

"Cool," I said, turning away from him to focus my thoughts on the game.

While the rest of the guys got amped up about the game, Russ and I looked out the window, totally silent.

🏀   🏀   🏀

When we got to Willamette Middle School, we filed off the bus.

"Here's your eraser," a Twinvader said, handing it back to Russ. "Thanks for letting me use it."

"Anytime," Russ said, tucking it back into its pouch. "Were you working on the assignment from Mr. Hollis?"

"No. One of the girls from our old math club e-mailed us a problem, and we were trying to solve it."

"Cool," Russ said. "You know, Lewis and Clark has a math club, too, and—"

"We're not interested," the other brother said from behind us.

"But it's a great group of people and—" Russ began, but he was cut off.

"Not interested. Come on, Marcus. We need to warm up."

Without another word, he nudged his twin and they took off up the path to the main door of the school.

"So, I guess Mitch is the bigger jerk," I said, glad to have cleared that up, anyway.

"I guess," Russ said quietly.

Once we were inside the school, we followed the sound of squeaking shoes to the gym. When we got there, we saw that the bleachers were practically full.

"Big crowd," I said quietly.

"We've had bigger," said one of the twins.

Why couldn't one of them always stand on the right or something? I'd mixed them up again!

"Back in Minnesota," the other one explained, "everyone comes to the games."

"They make signs, blow horns—"

"And dress in team colors," they both said at once.

Enough with the surround sound, I thought.

But the rest of the guys were leaning in to hear better, like they'd bought tickets to hear those bozos talk.

I mean, *come on*.

We dumped our stuff around the visitors' bench and started to warm up.

I dribbled a ball over to the free throw line and took a few shots, hearing the sounds of my teammates getting into game mode around me.

Whenever I checked over my shoulder, the Warriors looked pretty smooth. But who didn't look smooth during *drills*?

I glanced back at the Pioneers, who had about a hundred balls in the air at once, all bumping each other out of the basket.

Well, maybe *we* didn't look so smooth.

I noticed Mitch and Marcus weren't shooting with the rest of the guys and spotted them near center court. They were standing about ten feet apart, bounce-passing two balls between each other at turbo speed.

They didn't miss a single catch, and every pass was perfect. And the weird part was, neither one of them was even looking at the balls. They were staring into each other's eyes instead.

While I watched, they passed faster and faster, never missing a beat.

Where did they play last? A freakin' circus?

"Okay, that is seriously awesome," Nate said, from next to me.

Before I had a chance to say anything else, the ref blew his whistle and it was time to huddle up.

I was hoping Coach Baxter would start me this time, so I wouldn't have to be embarrassed by spending those first minutes on the bench.

But he put both of the Matthews brothers in instead.

After the huddle, I watched the rest of the guys run into their positions.

That's when I saw it.

I was shocked I hadn't noticed it on the bus.

Paul and Nate had both parted their hair like the new guys and molded it to their heads with goo.

Come on.

"What's with the hair?" I asked Russ.

He patted his. "Mine?"

"No, Nate's and Paul's. They *styled* theirs just like the Twinvaders'."

He glanced at them. "*Hmm.* Maybe it's to improve their aerodynamics."

I rolled my eyes. "This isn't NASA, Russ. It's freakin' middle-school basketball."

"Well," he said with a shrug, "you asked."

The Warriors took possession at the tip-off, and I realized that I should have seen their smooth drills as a warning.

Those guys knew what to do, and they did it well.

"Nice play," Russ said when a Warrior practically ran over Nate to make a basket.

"Geez, don't compliment the other team, Russ." I couldn't believe the stuff I still had to tell him about basketball.

"Well, it *was* a good play."

"So, wait for us to make a good one."

He didn't have to wait long.

Paul passed to a Matthews twin, who spun around and passed to his brother, who was in perfect position for a three-pointer.

"Yes!" a couple of our fellow benchwarmers shouted, jumping to their feet to cheer.

I tried to smile but I couldn't help wishing someone else had scored.

And I ended up wishing that a lot during the first quarter, when Mitch and Marcus racked up points like it was a video game instead of real life.

But the Warriors weren't giving up.

By the time Russ and I got in the game, the Pioneers were down six points and I was looking forward to closing the gap.

When I passed the Twinvaders coming off the court, I lifted a hand for a high five, and they both ignored it. I pretended to check my watch, so I wouldn't look like a total loser, but I didn't have a watch on.

Russ must have seen the guys diss me, so he lifted his hand for a high five from me instead.

Based on experience, I knew I was making a mistake, but I went for it.

Russ's hand missed mine and then we *both* looked like losers.

Great.

The ref blew his whistle and one of the Pioneers passed me the ball. I hauled down the court, dodging red jerseys all the way. I could hear the handful of our fans who'd made the trip cheering for me, and that got me pumped.

I had my chance at a basket and was just about to shoot when a Warrior reached over my back and shoved the ball to the side.

"You've gotta move faster, Owen!" Coach Baxter shouted from the bench.

I gritted my teeth and took off running so I could get the ball back. But I was too late.

Two points for the Warriors.

Ugh.

When I had my next chance at a shot, I choked and threw a total brick.

"Take your time, Owen," Coach called to me.

What did he want me to do? Speed up or slow down?

If I hadn't spent so much time on the bench, my playing wouldn't be so rusty. I just knew it.

Russ did okay, though. He made a couple of sweet jump shots, and I was totally proud of him.

By the time Coach pulled us out, the Pioneers were eight points ahead, thanks to nine points from Russ and four from me.

I reminded myself that four was better than none as I walked back to the bench.

But "better than none" didn't do much for me at the end of the game. We won, forty-eight to thirty-nine, but only six of the points were mine.

The Matthews twins walked out of there with thirty points between them.

When I got home that night, I grabbed my ball out of the garage so I could take some practice shots. I tried a few from the free throw line I'd marked on the concrete, and made most of them. I took a few more from the corner by the mailbox but didn't have as much luck.

I thought about some of the moves Mitch and Marcus had been showing off at practices and at the game.

I bounced the ball through my legs, like they had, slowly walking toward the street and passing it through on each step.

Not bad.

Figuring it wouldn't hurt to push myself, I tried to do the same thing while walking backward up the driveway.

It was way harder, and I lost control of the ball almost as many times as I banged it against the backs of my knees.

"You look just like M&M," Russ said, from behind me.

The ball bounced against my ankle and rolled onto the grass. "I wasn't trying to," I lied.

"It was a compliment," Russ said with a shrug. "They're really good."

"Yeah, well they aren't the first people on the planet to dribble like that."

"I didn't say they were."

"Lots of people do it."

"Fine," he said, shrugging again.

"Fine," I repeated, then picked up the ball and carried it into the garage.

I really didn't feel like practicing anymore.

"You know, I think one of them was going to high-five you at the game," Russ called after me.

"One of who? The Twinvaders?" I shook my head. "Nah, they both ignored me."

"I don't think so. I'm pretty sure it was Marcus who moved toward you, then Mitch kind of blocked him."

I couldn't help snorting. "You're seeing things, Russ. Mitch might be the bigger jerk, but they're *both* jerks."

"I'm not so sure," he said.

"Yeah, well I am," I told him, starting toward the door.

"I'm just saying that Marcus might be okay."

That was the last thing I needed to hear. "It's official," I muttered, as I walked back inside. "The whole team's been brainwashed."

⚫ 🏀 ✳

Just before dinner that night, I was washing my hands in the bathroom sink when I glanced at myself in the mirror. I turned off the faucet and let the water drip off my fingers as I studied my reflection.

Curious, I lifted one hand up to the top of my head and started to push the hair to one side.

It wouldn't stay, so I ran the faucet again and dipped one of Dad's little black combs under the water, then pushed the hair to the side.

I used the comb to make a perfect part and was just about to take a good, long look at myself when the door swung open.

"Oops!" Mom gasped. "Sorry, O, I didn't know you were in here." She started to close the door again, but stopped partway. "Hey, I like what you've done with your hair. Very cute."

Cute?

I leaned closer to the mirror. She was right, it wasn't a bad look.

I jerked backward.

What was I thinking?

I didn't want Twinvader hair.

I didn't want Twinvader *anything*.

And I definitely didn't want to look *cute*.

I dropped the comb back into the drawer and messed up my hair with my hands.

If I wasn't careful, I'd be sucked into the Matthews brothers' trap, just like the rest of the Pioneers.

And I didn't want that most of all.

At dinner, Dad congratulated us on our game.

"The streak continues, huh?" he said, passing me the carrots.

"Yeah," I muttered, scooping a bunch onto my plate.

"Wow," Dad said. "Now *that's* enthusiasm."

"I thought you'd be thrilled with another win," Mom said.

"I would, if *we'd* won."

They both looked totally confused, and I guess I couldn't blame them.

"The Matthews twins," Russ explained, once he'd swallowed a mouthful of salmon. "They're dominating the team."

"Dominating, huh?" Dad asked.

"Yeah, *dominating*," I said, trying not to sound ticked off but failing.

"But everyone's getting court time, right?" Dad asked.

"Yeah," I admitted. "But Russ and I have been starting on the bench lately."

"Somebody has to start on the bench," Mom said.

Like that helped.

"Yeah, but it used to be somebody *else*," I said, passing the carrots to Russ.

"You know," Dad said. "You guys are looking at these twins as threats instead of allies. And that's a big mistake."

"What do you mean?" Russ asked.

Dad swallowed a mouthful. "You already had a team who was great together, right?"

"Yeah, back in the good old days," I muttered.

"And now you've added two more solid players to the roster, which will make your great team even greater."

I nodded, even though I didn't totally agree. "Uh-huh."

"So, why are you worrying about how you start? You should be thinking about how you finish."

"We *are* winning," Russ said quietly.

"No," I told both of them. "The Matthews twins are winning. The rest of us are just decoration."

"Then you need to step up your game, Owen," Dad said. "Be a part of what they're doing instead of treating them like your enemies. If they're making most of the plays, help them make even more."

"Are you kidding me?" I choked.

"Hey, a good assist is as valuable as the basket itself."

Yeah, right.

"They don't need assists from us," I told him.

"They're like a full team on their own," Russ agreed.

Dad laughed. "Two players can never do more than five, you guys."

I gave up on trying to convince him. He just didn't get it.

At the next practice, I was ready to do my best, because that was all I really *could* do.

But when Chris showed up wearing a Timberwolves T-shirt, I got distracted.

"What's that about?" I asked, pointing at it. "Since when do you like Minnesota?"

"They're not bad," he said, shrugging.

"Seriously?" I couldn't believe he'd joined the stupid fan club! "Why don't you start combing your hair like the Matthewses', too? Maybe you can be triplets together."

Coach blew his whistle before Chris could say anything.

For the whole practice, I concentrated on playing as hard as I could so that when the Hogarth game rolled around, I'd be ready to make a difference.

But I couldn't keep one question out of my mind: What if I finally had my chance to face off with Dante Powers and I was stuck on the bench?

RUSSELL

Divisibility Rules

The Pioneers' winning streak should have been enough to keep Owen bouncing off the walls with happiness, but all I heard about for the next few days was the upcoming game against Hogarth.

I'd never seen Dante Powers before, but I'd heard plenty. In the past I would have written it all off as exaggeration, but now that I'd played with the Mitch and Marcus, I knew that it was possible for someone my age to be extremely good.

But even the best player on a team had to take a break sometime, didn't he?

"Don't you see?" I said to Owen on the way home from school one afternoon. "When Dante's on the bench, that's when we'll strike."

Owen shook his head. "No, that's when the *Twinvaders* will strike."

I sighed. "You've got to get them out of your head, O."

It was advice I should have been giving myself. Science class had turned into my least favorite period, next to math, where M&M continued to outwit everybody (including Mr. Hollis) without scrap paper, calculators, or more than a few seconds of thought.

I became almost obsessed with watching them in the classroom, and I was surprised when my frustration turned to fascination. Then, totally unexpectedly, I was able to tell them apart!

Marcus very rarely raised his hand in class, but when Mitch raised his, Marcus was always ready to back him up or complete a thought. Marcus took the notes while Mitch did the talking.

In the hallways, Mitch always walked slightly ahead, leading the way for his twin. I'd never noticed it before, but I had the feeling it had been happening all along.

And even though they seemed to have the same expressions on their faces most of the time, I realized that Marcus was quicker to smile than his brother. He was also the one to fix things if Mitch offended someone or sounded kind of rude.

The way Marcus stayed in the background and kept things running smoothly for himself and his brother was strangely familiar.

It didn't take long for me to realize that Marcus was a lot like me.

Sensing that we had things in common, I tried to speak to him between classes, but Mitch was always there to step in and break it up.

I got the distinct feeling that Mitch didn't need anyone else. He wanted to be part of a twosome, and no more.

$$\times \quad \div \quad +$$

I might have been figuring out the differences between the Matthews twins, but that didn't mean I'd abandoned my dream of being in sync with Owen.

I'd tried dressing exactly the same on the court, right down to the Nike swooshes on our socks. I matched his stride when we walked and tried anything else I could think of, but none of it worked.

On the way home one afternoon, I gave it another try.

"Close your eyes for a second," I told Owen.

"What now? I'm walking, Russ."

"Just stop where you are and close your eyes."

"What for?" he asked suspiciously.

"Can't you just trust me?"

He sighed, but did what I'd asked.

I closed my eyes, too, and tried to clear my mind of everything but one thought. I made it really easy for him by picturing an orange basketball. Nothing else; just the ball.

"Okay," I said. "What are you thinking about right this second?"

"Right now?"

"Yes. Just blurt it out."

"I'm thinking about dipping a Cheeto into chocolate pudding and trying to decide whether it would taste awesome or totally disgusting."

I opened my eyes. "Are you joking?"

He opened his as well. "No, why?"

"Never mind. Let's try this again. Close your eyes and picture one object. Get rid of everything else and just picture that one object."

"This is stupid."

I waited until he closed his eyes, then closed my own. I cleared my mind again and waited for something to pop into it.

After a couple of seconds, it did. There was a picture of a scoreboard in my head, red numbers bright and flashing.

"What are you picturing?" I asked.

"A banana split."

I opened my eyes again. "*Owen.*"

"What?" He shrugged. "I'm hungry."

"Never mind." I started walking again, irritated.

"What was I supposed to say?" Owen asked, jogging to catch up with me.

"It doesn't matter."

"You wouldn't be looking all ticked off if it didn't matter."

"I don't look ticked off."

"Well, I'm the only one of us who can actually see your face, and I'm telling you that you look ticked off. What's the problem?"

I sighed. "I'm trying to get in sync with you, Owen. I've spent the last few days trying to create a mental bond like M&M have."

"What? We already have a bond."

"Not like theirs. They dress alike—"

"Is *that* why you keep asking me what I'm wearing?"

"They anticipate each other's moves, finish each other's sentences, share the same thoughts—"

"Hold on, Russ," he said, grabbing my arm. "First of all, the mind-reading stuff is seriously creepy, okay? And second, do you really want to be like those guys?"

"Why not? You do."

"No, I don't. I want to *play* like them, but all the other stuff is just weird."

"It's not . . . weird," I told him. "It's amazing."

"Yeah, like unicorns and all your other sci-fi stuff." He shook his head. "I want to be out on the court, making awesome plays with you, Russ. Not reading your mind like a freakin' fortune-teller on the walk home."

I couldn't help smiling about the awesome plays *with me* part.

Maybe the rest of it wasn't so important.

✕ ÷ ✛

When I went to my next Masters of the Mind meeting at Jason's house, I was the last to arrive.

"Here he is," Nitu said, smiling. "It's so unlike you to be tardy, we were going to form a Russ search party."

"Sorry about that," I said. "I had to finish a couple of things at home."

"*Hmm*," Jason said, raising one eyebrow. "Not a rhyming response."

"Is everything okay?" Sara asked.

"It's fine," I told her, then looked at each of my team members. "I'm fine."

It took a couple of minutes to convince them, but when I did, we moved on to Masters business.

"Regionals are coming up fast," Sara said. "I know we want to have a new team member in place with time left to practice."

"Yeah, but I haven't been able to find a single candidate," Jason said, sighing.

"Neither have I," I told them.

"I have," Nitu told the group. "Well, two of them, actually."

"Seriously?" I asked, surprised. She hadn't mentioned anything to me.

"Yes. I think we should ask the Matthews twins."

I practically choked on my orange juice. "What? Why?"

She stared at me, like it was a ridiculous question. "Russ,

you've seen them in math class. They've always got a differ-ent or unusual angle to explore."

"That sounds like Masters of the Mind," Jason said, nodding.

Nitu continued, "The whole point of this team is thinking outside the box, and I don't think those two can think *inside* of it."

"They sound perfect," Sara said, smiling.

"Then why does Russ look like that?" Jason asked.

"Like what?" I asked.

"Like you just drank lumpy milk."

Sara and Nitu gave me a closer look.

"You do," Nitu said, then frowned. "This isn't about the twins playing basketball, is it?"

"No," I said, firmly. "Well, maybe a little bit. You see, they've totally taken over that team and I—"

"Don't want them to take over this one," Nitu finished for me.

"Yes," I admitted. From my observations, I felt that Mar-cus had the potential to be a good guy, but together? M&M were a total threat.

I tried to describe their bond and their ability to com-municate without speaking. I tried to explain how quickly they were taking over the Pioneers.

"This isn't basketball," Nitu reasoned. "You can't worry about stuff like that."

"But he is," Sara reminded her.

"What if we just asked one of them to join?" Jason suggested. "Then there's no doubling up."

I thought about how Mitch wouldn't even stand in line one body apart from his twin.

"One won't do it without the other," I told them. "They do absolutely everything together."

We discussed the possibility for a little while longer and with every passing minute, I was more certain it wouldn't work.

"Well," Nitu said, once we'd run out of things to say, "It can't hurt to ask."

✖   ÷   ✚

At the next Pioneers practice I didn't even look at the twins while I ran my warm-up laps. I didn't glance at their matching shoes as they passed me or watch them make perfect shots. I focused on my own drills and playing as much as I could.

But it wasn't easy.

They were amazing, and at one time or another every Pioneer stood still to watch them for at least a few seconds.

Every Pioneer except Owen, anyway. He managed to have his back to them at all times.

In math class, I concentrated on my own work. When an M came up with an idea I hadn't considered or a way of solving a problem that no one else in class would have imagined, I simply accepted it and moved on.

I found myself behaving differently in class as a result. Even though I had a feeling that Marcus was human, I felt uncomfortable around Mitch.

I rarely raised my hand to answer questions, and when the conversation turned toward one of their ideas, I ended up doodling in the pages of my notebook.

"Russell," Nitu whispered to me. "Listen."

"I *am* listening," I whispered back.

But I didn't like what I was hearing.

Science class wasn't much different. The power duo shared rock samples their dad had brought back from geology trips to Asia and Africa. They had original diagrams he'd drawn, which had been published in university textbooks. They even brought in rock candy for a class treat on the last day of our geology section.

Some days I dealt with my jealousy and uncertainty pretty well. Other days, I hated them.

✕ ÷ ✚

As the Hogarth game got closer, the Pioneers started to get more excited than I'd ever seen them. In the cafeteria, they were almost too busy talking to eat.

"I think we can take them," Chris said.

"We totally can," Paul agreed, nodding.

"Okay, remember that we're talking about a perfect record here. And Dante Powers," Nate warned them.

"That's true," Nicky Chu said. "He's not exactly a regular player."

"But the rest of them are," I said, thinking about what I'd tried to explain to Owen. "I mean, there's no one else on the team who stands out as a serious threat, is there?"

"No," Nate admitted. "But Dante Powers is like five players rolled into one."

I thought back to what Dad had said about two players not being able to do the work of a whole team.

"As I mentioned to Owen the other day, I think the key is for us to attack when Dante is on the bench."

"Which will give us about three minutes," Nate said. "That kid is *never* on the bench."

"Have you ever seen them play?" I asked.

"Well, no."

"Then how do you know?"

Nate shrugged. "Anybody who scores more than thirty points in a game isn't riding the bench."

He had a point there.

I was about to respond when Nitu appeared next to me. She said hello to everyone, then quietly asked, "I was thinking about the Matthews twins. Maybe it would be best if you were the one who asked them about joining the Masters."

"Me?" I choked.

"Well, you play basketball with them, so you know them better than the rest of us."

"I don't play *with* them," I whispered back. "I play on the same court at the same time while wearing the same uniform. But that's where the familiarity ends."

"That again?" she said, and sighed. "Russell, you're being ridiculous about this."

"No, I'm not, I'm—"

"The most logical person to invite them. It doesn't even matter which one you ask. It's totally your choice."

Somehow, that didn't make me feel any better. "Fine," I finally said.

"Cool." Nitu gave my shoulder a squeeze and headed back to her table.

"What was that about?" Owen asked, looking suspicious.

"I'm supposed to invite one of the Matthews twins to join Masters of the Mind."

He paused, then said, "You're kidding."

"I wish."

"Are you going to do it?" he asked.

I sighed. "Not right away."

After all, there was a chance that some genius with time on her hands would fall from the sky and beg to join the team before Regionals.

It might not have been a *good* chance, but it was still possible.

I tuned out the rest of the lunchroom conversation, which had switched back to the big game. Part of me wondered what we would talk about when it was finally over.

Hopefully what a great win it had been.

We still had to make it through a couple of days before we played Hogarth, and the Pioneers were like a big bag of firecrackers, waiting to be lit.

I should have known one of us would get burned.

The Matchup

The day had finally come.

I turned off my alarm clock and wiped all the crusty junk out of my eyes. I was pretty sure I'd had about eleven minutes of sleep, after lying awake and staring at the ceiling for most of the night, pulling on blankets and throwing them off, over and over again.

I stood up, then waited for my brain to catch up with my body.

Game day.

Owen Evans vs. Dante Powers.

For real.

I stretched and walked to the bathroom, feeling nervous. I wished I could fast-forward through the whole day, straight to the tip-off. I wished I knew what was going to happen.

I spent my whole shower with my eyes closed, picturing myself being carried on the shoulders of my teammates after defeating the Huskies by the most insane lead in Pioneers' history.

I was about to play against the best kid in the state and hopefully beat him.

How cool was that?

I met up with Russ in the kitchen, where he was eating a banana while Mom packed our lunches.

"Big day," Russ said, looking up from the textbook he was studying.

"Big *win*," I corrected, pouring myself a glass of milk and making my way to the tower of toast at the center of the table. I took a couple of pieces and coated them with crunchy peanut butter. My favorite.

"I hope so," Russ said, taking another bite of banana.

He already had strands of it stuck to his braces and I hated to think what his smile would look like by the time he finished eating it.

"It's gonna happen, Russ. Hogarth is going down, just like everyone else we've played this season."

"Seriously?"

"We're on a roll, and nothing's going to stop us."

"Not even Dante Powers?" he asked, looking happy to hear it.

"*Especially* not Dante Powers."

When I got to school, the clock stopped.

Well, it felt like it, anyway.

Every class seemed twice as long as normal and even study hall dragged. By the time the lunch bell rang, I felt like I'd been sitting in social studies for six weeks solid.

"So," Chris said, "you guys ready for the game?"

"Definitely," Paul said, nodding. "I think we can take them."

"I'm with Paul," I told him and the rest of the table. "It's our time. We're having the best season ever and a bunch of hype isn't going to mess that up."

"Dante Powers isn't hype," Nate said. "He's a legend."

"He's a twelve-year-old, just like us. And he'll need a break sometime," I told him, thinking about what Russ had said. "That's what we need to concentrate on."

"I wonder what Coach has planned for a starting lineup," Chris said.

"I think he should stick with what we've been doing," Paul said. "It's working for us, isn't it?"

"Not for all of us," I muttered.

"What?" Chris asked.

"Nothing," I lied, concentrating on my sandwich.

And thinking about being stuck on the bench was all it took to bring on a bad mood.

After lunch, Russ walked with me to my locker.

"You've got to snap out of it, Owen," he said.

"Snap out of what?"

"This funk. Your attitude about the game."

"Look, I already know what's going to happen, and I can't help feeling crummy about it, okay?"

Russ frowned. "You don't know what's going to happen."

"Come on, Russ. You're a smart guy. You know we're going to warm the bench while Mitch and Marcus wow everyone again."

He shook his head. "You can't think like that."

"Yeah, I can."

"Owen," he said, grabbing my arm to stop me from walking. "I'm serious."

"So am I. I've been looking forward to this game all season and it's already ruined."

"No, it isn't. In a couple of hours, the ref will blow his whistle and anything can happen. If you don't start, you'll still play at some point. And whenever you're out there, you have to play as hard as you can to make those minutes count."

"But—"

"And when you're on the bench, you've got to do the things you've always done, like cheer the guys on and show your Pioneer spirit."

Come on.

"Russ, I—"

"I'll see you on the bus," he said, walking toward the stairs.

My brother's words stuck with me for the whole afternoon.

At first I thought he was out of his mind and tried to forget the whole conversation, but then I realized that Russ was right.

I couldn't predict what was going to happen when the ref blew his whistle.

And if I started on the bench, that didn't mean I'd stay there for the whole game. I'd have my chance at Dante Powers and it was up to me to make it count, no matter how many minutes I had on the court.

After all, ESPN highlights were only a few seconds apiece, max.

And that meant that any time I had on the court could be enough to make something awesome happen.

I finally made it through the afternoon, and the next thing I knew, the Pioneers and I were on a yellow bus, heading for Hogarth Middle School.

It was time to attack the mighty Huskies and hope we didn't get bitten.

It was time to take on Dante Powers.

"We're going to make history," I told Russ and the rest of the guys. It felt good to have my "Pioneer spirit" back.

"Or we're going to *be* history," one of the guys said.

"Come on," I said. "We can totally do this. We've won four games in a row."

"And they've won six," Nate said.

"Seven, actually," Russ said, taking his nose out of his sci-fi novel.

I don't know how he did it. If I read in a moving car, I'd puke for sure.

Mitch and Marcus turned around at the exact same time.

"What's so great about . . . what's his name again?" one of them asked.

"Dante Powers," we all said at once.

"The kid might as well be in high school," Nicky Chu said.

"More like college," I corrected. "He holds the record for most points scored in a single game for the whole state."

"What's the record?" one of them asked.

"I just told you. Most points scored in a single—"

"No." He sighed. "I meant how many points."

"Over thirty," I said, then waited for their jaws to drop. But they didn't.

"How many, exactly?" one asked.

"Thirty-one," I announced.

They looked at each other and shrugged. "We've scored more than that."

I practically choked. "What?"

"How many?" Russ asked, forgetting all about his book.

"Thirty-five."

"Get out of here," Nicky Chu said, waving his hand like they were kidding and he was onto them.

"He's thirty-five," one of the twins said, pointing at the other. "I'm thirty-seven."

"In a single game?" Paul gasped.

"Yeah." The twin shrugged. "Not the *same* game, but yeah, in single games."

"That's unbelievable," Nate whispered.

"Believe it," the Twinvaders said, killing the conversation for the rest of the trip.

When we got to Hogarth, I wasn't nearly as excited as I'd hoped to be.

I couldn't stop thinking about those high scores and wondering how long it would be before the Matthews brothers made over thirty-five points in a Pioneers game. Sure, Coach was all about sharing court time, but if they racked up points, Russ and I would be doomed to the bench forever.

I followed the rest of the guys into the school, my bag of gear feeling like it weighed a hundred pounds.

"What's wrong now?" Russ asked, as we walked past a wall of lockers.

"Thirty-seven points."

Russ cleared his throat, which he always did when he was nervous. "That was only one time. And the other one only scored thirty-five."

Was he kidding?

"Russ, what's the highest number of points *you've* scored in a game?"

"Nineteen," he said, adjusting his glasses.

"Exactly."

"But you've scored twenty-five."

"Twenty," I corrected.

"That's still good, you know."

"It's almost half of theirs, Russ."

We walked past the Huskies' trophy case, which was filled with pictures, newspaper stories, and trophies.

Lots of them.

And that's when I started to get really nervous. We were going up against the team with the best record in the county, so there was no guarantee we'd win or even come close.

There was also no guarantee that either Mitch or Marcus wouldn't break his own record.

What if one of them scored over thirty points against Dante Powers?

Now *that* would be making history.

And what if I had to watch it happen from my new home on the bench?

The thought made me want to puke up my Pioneer spirit.

"Owen?"

"Yeah?" I turned toward the gym.

"You look kind of pale."

"I'm fine, Russ."

"But you're—"

"I'm fine," I snapped.

But I wasn't.

Instead of letting us use the girls' locker room, like most schools did, Hogarth made us get changed for the game in the boys' bathroom.

"This is lame." Paul pulled on his jersey and banged his elbow on a paper towel dispenser.

"They're just trying to psych us out," Nicky Chu told him. "They want to go into the game feeling like they've got the edge."

"They *do* have the edge," Nate said. "They've got Dante freakin' Powers."

"He's just a kid," Russ said quietly, "like us."

"A kid who's already been on TV," Paul said.

"We were on TSPN," a voice said from behind me.

"What?" Nate choked, turning to face the Matthews twins. "How did a couple of twelve-year-olds make it onto the biggest sports channel in the country?"

"No," a twin said. "TSPN."

"Hold the phone." I lifted a hand to stop him. "What the heck is TSPN?"

"A Twin Cities sports show," the brothers said together. "Hosted by Matt Larson."

I checked the rest of the guys' faces and they looked as clueless as I was.

"Matt Larson," one of them said again, like repeating the name would make a difference.

"Never mind." His brother sighed. "Let's go warm up, Mitch."

Aha! I was back on track. I knew which one was which.

But that lasted for only about ten seconds. As soon as they left the bathroom, fully geared up, I had them mixed up again.

Great.

When I and the rest of the Pioneers walked into the gym, the bleachers were totally packed with fans wearing black and gray, waving signs, and shouting their support for their team.

Their undefeated team.

I wondered if the sinking feeling in my stomach was the same thing visitors felt when they came to play at Lewis and Clark.

I watched the Huskies warming up and looked for Dante Powers. But I didn't see him anywhere.

I couldn't decide if I was relieved or disappointed.

"What if Powers isn't playing?" I said out loud.

"We win," Chris said with a shrug.

I knew he was right, but would it still feel like a historic victory if we beat the Huskies in their own house *without* their star player?

Probably not.

But would I take it?

Definitely.

I watched Mitch and Marcus pass the ball back and forth to each other, under the net.

The truth was, if we *did* end up losing the game, I kind of wanted to see the two of them go down in flames against Dante Powers.

"There he is," Chris whispered, pointing to the locker room door.

"Yup." I sighed.

He wasn't a tall kid, or loaded with muscles. He didn't have a wild haircut or wear flashier shoes than anybody else. He was the kind of guy you'd never notice.

Until he played.

Dante pulled off his team hoodie and lifted one hand in the air. Within about half a second, one of his teammates threw him a ball. He bounced it a couple of times, then passed it around his back a bunch of times, really fast.

"What a show-off," I said, more jealous than I'd ever been.

"It's for the cameras," Paul said, pointing to the far side of the gym.

I followed his finger and there they were. Two news cameras, both focused on Dante.

"No way," I whispered.

What if Hogarth beat us with cameras rolling?

We had to win.

Just like I expected, Russ and I shared our new spot on the bench for the first few minutes of the game while the Twinvaders lit up the scoreboard.

Instead of going down in flames, they were on fire, right from the tip-off.

I watched them race up and down the court, never looking tired or out of breath. I watched them pass the ball without looking or probably even thinking about it.

"Here we go," I said with a sigh.

After one of the twins scored again, the Huskies' coach put Powers in.

The whole crowd went quiet, like they knew they were about to see the best show of their lives.

I held my breath as he dribbled down the court, looking totally cool and calm. He dodged around Chris, no problem, then paused to bounce the ball between his legs, backward and forward, like Mitch and Marcus did.

I glanced at the cameras, which were glued to him.

Then he dribbled forward again, keeping an eye on the basket.

I wondered if he would go for the three-pointer, knowing he would sink the ball. Or would he work his way through the Pioneers, spinning, pivoting, and dribbling like a pro?

It turned out he didn't have a chance to do either.

Negative Integers

I watched in absolute amazement as the legendary Dante Powers spun around, ready to take a shot, only to come face-to-chests with M&M.

With four arms going after the ball, he didn't stand a chance, and in just a few seconds, the brothers managed to gain possession. Half a second after that, they were running in tandem down the court, smiling.

"They tag-teamed him," Owen said quietly. His mouth hung open.

"Smart," I said, watching them score yet another basket.

Owen snorted. "You've got to stop complimenting the enemy, Russ."

"They're on our team," I reminded him.

"Whatever."

We only had to wait about ten minutes to get into the game, but the way Owen carried on about the unfairness of it all, it felt more like an hour.

When he finally pulled us off the bench, Coach Baxter put us in for Chris and Nate instead of Mitch and Marcus.

"They're too good for the sidelines?" Owen muttered as we jogged onto the court.

"They're playing really well," I said, looking for a bright side in what was turning out to be a dark afternoon.

"Totally not the point, Russ."

The ref blew his whistle and Paul passed the ball to one of the Matthews twins, who passed to the other. They dribbled down the court together, only pausing to toss the ball back and forth over Dante Powers's head before scoring. Again.

"There's a whole team out here," Owen muttered. "Let's get our passing game going, you freakin' ball hogs."

I wondered if he'd already forgotten his own brief stint as a ball hog. Just last month, he'd practically destroyed the team by turning the Pioneers into a one-man show.

"Tell them when you're open," I suggested.

Owen shook his head. "Whatever."

But the next time an M had possession, Owen *did* shout that he was open, loud enough to be heard in the parking lots not only of Hogarth, but the Safeway three blocks away.

But Marcus and Mitch kept the ball to themselves.

And scored.

Again.

"This is a joke," Owen muttered. "A total joke."

Dante Powers dribbled up the court, and when Owen tried to steal the ball, Dante used all kinds of fancy footwork and clever dribbling to stop him. After a few flustered seconds, Owen ended up chasing him toward the basket but didn't make it in time.

My brother was fast, but not *that* fast.

Dante jumped in the air and almost touched the rim with his fingertips as he tipped the ball into the basket.

The crowd went wild.

"Nice defense," one of the Matthews twins told Owen, sarcastically.

"Yeah," the other one said. "It's like Swiss cheese."

"Full of holes," they both said.

I could tell by the expression on Owen's face that he was trying to think of the perfect comeback. And I knew from experience that it wouldn't happen until at least dinnertime, when it was way too late.

"Come on, O," I said, slapping him on the back. "Let's focus on the game, okay?"

"What do you think I'm doing?"

"Letting them get to you. The real enemies are the Huskies. Let's show them what we're made of."

Unfortunately, we showed them that we were made of sloppy moves and short fuses.

I don't know whether it was all the buildup to playing Dante Powers or feeling a sense of competition with the other twins, but Owen and I were even less in sync than usual.

His passes were too fast and low for me to catch, and he started taking wild shots instead of letting M&M sink baskets.

And worst of all? Dante Powers practically danced around my brother every chance he got. His footwork was phenomenal, his ball handling brilliant, and if I didn't know better, I'd think I was watching an NBA superstar instead of a twelve-year-old kid.

"Maybe you can get an autograph after the game," Owen hissed at me, after I watched Dante score another incredible basket.

"He's pretty amazing," I said, watching the star high-five his teammates.

"He's the enemy, Russ."

"Sure, but—"

"The *enemy*," he said, more firmly.

But within a matter of minutes, Owen was back to finding enemies in other places. Like our own roster.

We'd both been pulled back to the bench, which was kind of a relief. There was nothing fun about letting the team down, and Owen and I had done way too much of that in just a few minutes.

"I can't get it together," Owen said quietly.

"Maybe you need to relax a bit."

His entire body seemed stiff and awkward on the court, whether he was dribbling, shooting, or finding an opening.

"Relax?" he scoffed. "Are you kidding me, Russ? This is the most important game of the year."

"So far."

"Yeah, so far. And I'm trying hard to make my minutes count, but I'm blowing it."

"You're not blowing it," I lied, to save his feelings.

He sighed. "Nothing I do is working. I can't catch a break."

I used a towel to wipe the perspiration from the back of my neck. "You'll have another chance."

As we watched from the bench, Marcus and Mitch's perfect passes never faltered.

It struck me that there was almost a science to what they were doing on the court. It was like the ball was magnetic, drawn from one twin to the other, never stopping for anything in between. And when they tag-teamed Dante Powers a second time, then a third, they looked like the model of an atom in my science classroom. Dante was a proton, holding the basketball neutron while the twins circled like electrons.

Owen saw things differently.

"It's like a couple of guys are out on the court, hogging the clock, while two awesome players are stuck riding the bench."

I glanced to my right, then my left.

"I'm talking about *you and me*."

"You think I'm an awesome player?" I asked, surprised.

"Yeah. I mean, not as awesome as me, but we make a good team, Russ."

It was true. We might not have been playing well at that particular moment, but Owen and I were a good team when we communicated with each other.

"We do, don't we?" I couldn't help smiling.

"But not while we're stuck on the sidelines."

"Sure," I said, nodding.

"So you know what that means, right?" Owen asked, raising an eyebrow.

"Yes," I said, thinking about all the efforts I'd made to try to get in sync with my brother. Perhaps the reason it hadn't worked was because I didn't fully explain what I was doing. We weren't working on it *together*.

"We need to align our minds," I told him.

"No," Owen said, and sighed. "First of all, I don't even know what that means, and second? It doesn't matter because you're wrong."

"How can you say—"

"We need to take down the Twinvaders."

At first, I couldn't believe what I was hearing. Then I remembered how Owen had thrown my Nikes into a Dumpster to end the competition between us on the court. And I recalled the brainstorming session we'd had when I wanted to remove Arthur Richardson the Third from my Masters of the Mind team. Owen was the one who'd come up with the successful—and sinister—scheme.

There was no doubt that he was formulating another diabolical plan.

"You want to sabotage them?" I asked, still kind of hoping I was wrong, despite the glint in his eye.

"Yeah."

"You want to sabotage our own *teammates*," I said, just to be sure we were on the same page.

"Yes. We take them down and everything goes back to the way it was. Back when we were the team that had been together forever."

"Owen, I've only been on the Pioneers for a month."

"Well, you're a special case."

A few minutes earlier, I might have considered that a compliment.

"But M&M are part of the team now."

Owen rolled his eyes. "Barely. And look how they're taking over."

He had a point, there. They were dominating the court *and* the classroom. When I really thought about it, I had to admit I didn't like it either.

But was that a good enough reason to "take them down"?

I watched Mitch and Marcus perform yet another alley-oop, over the legendary Dante Powers's head.

Perhaps it was.

"What kind of a takedown are you planning?" I asked quietly.

Owen smiled and I half expected him to rub his hands together like a movie villain.

"I'm working on it. I'll fill you in when I've figured out the details."

"Okay," I told him, fighting off my doubts. "Keep me posted."

Coach blew his whistle and put me and Owen in the game to replace the Matthews twins. When they passed us, they didn't raise their hands for high fives, but Marcus nodded in my direction.

I had a sinking feeling about Owen's sabotage.

✖ ÷ ✚

That night, I set the table while Dad finished making a meal he called Hodge Podge. The mixture of chicken, mushrooms, and gravy over rice was one of the dishes our family ate when Mom wanted a break from cooking and told Dad that hot dogs were out of the question.

The other dishes were grilled-cheese sandwiches and spaghetti. Dad's menu was pretty limited.

"So, the streak is over," he said, as he stirred the chicken mixture in a pot.

Owen told Dad we lost to Hogarth right before he stormed upstairs to take what had to have been the longest shower in Evans family history. In fact, the water was still running and I was pretty sure the top floor of the house was a cloud of steam.

"The guys seem to think we can get another one started," I told Dad.

"That's the right attitude. There's always the next game. So, that Dante Powers character turned out to be everything you'd heard?"

"And more," I said with a sigh.

"The new guys couldn't stop him?"

I counted out the silverware and set each place. "They slowed him down, but stopping him was impossible."

"Pretty impressive," Dad said, then scooped a bit of his stew out to taste. He added some pepper. "Judging by his mood, I'm guessing your brother didn't have the game of his life."

"Not quite," I said.

Owen's playing was the worst I'd ever seen from him. The more frustrated he got, the less focus he had. Coach had benched him for the whole last quarter.

"What about you?" Dad asked.

"What about me?"

"How did you play?"

"Not as well as usual," I told him.

Dad stirred the pot a couple more times, then turned the temperature down to a simmer. "And why do you think that is?"

"I don't know." I shrugged. "There was a lot of buildup to this game. Everyone was nervous and—"

"Everyone but the twins?"

I nodded.

"Why not?"

"I'm not sure." I thought about it for a moment, as I laid out the napkins. "They don't really seem to be affected by anything." Every time I'd seen them, whether it was on the court, in the hallways, or in class, they'd been completely calm, like they didn't have a care in the world.

I wished I could feel the same way.

As I finished setting the table, I thought about the confidence of the Matthews twins and where they got it. I'd never been a new kid in school, but I'd always thought it would be kind of frightening. Yet from the second they arrived at Lewis and Clark, those two hadn't seemed nervous at all. *Hmm.*

Dad asked me to knock on the bathroom door and tell Owen to finish up in the shower while we still had water in the tank.

As I climbed the stairs, I thought about how I'd never seen M&M apart.

Ever.

Maybe their confidence came from each other.

And the more I thought about it, the more that made sense.

I reached the landing at the top of the stairs and as soon

as I knocked on the door, Owen turned off the water. He must have known he was pushing the limits.

"Dinner's just about ready," I told him through the door.

"Cool," he said, and I knew he must be feeling a little better.

I waited for him in his room, sitting at his desk and wondering for the hundredth time where all his study materials were. It seemed as though every place that should have been filled with pencils, paper, erasers, and everything else he'd need to do his homework was loaded with Blazer gear instead.

His chair was tilted back in a position that was better for daydreaming than hitting the books, and there was enough leftover Halloween candy scattered around that my teeth ached just looking at it.

I'd tried getting in sync with Owen in a lot of different ways, but being alone in his room gave me an idea.

I put on his favorite Blazer cap, then leaned back in the chair, gazing at the Blazers poster on the wall. But I still didn't feel like I was in his head yet, so I looked around for more gear.

I lifted his favorite hoodie from his bed and put it on, amazed at how short the arms were. I always forgot that I had the height advantage. Then again, Owen had the muscle—the body of the sweatshirt was huge on me.

I settled into his chair and closed my eyes.

"What are you doing?" Owen's voice asked from behind me.

I spun around to face him, surprised. "Nothing, I was just—"

"Boys! Dinner!" Dad shouted from downstairs.

"Never mind," Owen said, reaching for another Blazer hoodie. He slipped it over his head and led the way out of his room.

"I'm calling the center cushion for the game tonight," he said over his shoulder on the way downstairs.

"Fine," I said, glad to see him in a better mood.

Unfortunately, it didn't last very long.

OWEN

Offensive Rebound

My stomach was full of what had to be the best Hodge Podge ever, the headache I'd had from the game was washed away in the shower, and when I sat down on the center cushion with a bowl of chips in my lap, ready to share it with Dad and Russell, I was almost back to feeling good. Or normal, anyway.

And I know that sounds totally nuts because we *lost the game*.

After weeks of looking forward to taking on Dante Powers, I'd played one of the worst games of my life, so I'd been super ticked off on the way home.

It didn't hit me until I got into the shower that even though we had lost, something awesome had happened.

I hadn't stopped Dante in his tracks, but neither had

Mitch and Marcus. They hadn't been carried out of the gym on Pioneer shoulders.

We'd *all* blown it.

And that brought a smile to my face.

I glanced at Russ, who looked totally confused by my good mood.

"We're probably down to the last few minutes of the news," Dad said, flipping the channel to twelve. "Ahh, the sports report."

I looked up at the TV and my whole body went stiff.

No way.

Dante Powers was on our screen, dribbling like he was born doing it while some guy chased him around, waving his arms like a freakin' windmill.

And that guy was *me*.

"No way," I whispered, out loud this time.

"We'll be right back with the story of a local basketball phenom right after this," a woman's voice said.

Dad turned to me. "That looked like—"

"It was," I told him.

I knew I'd been a train wreck at the game, but I had no idea I looked *that* bad.

I'd waited my whole stinkin' life to get on TV and when I finally made it, they showed the worst moments of the worst game of my life?

I mean, *come on*.

And while I was being totally outplayed by Dante

Powers, my twin "teammates" were standing in the background and doing nothing to help me.

They were total jerks.

"Hey, you looked great out there," Dad said, during a commercial for Ford trucks. I wished one would plow through the wall right that second and run me over.

"Dad, don't," I begged.

"I'm serious."

I waited for the Dante Powers story to come on, and as much as I hoped they wouldn't do it, the news people showed the same clip again.

In slow motion.

It didn't look like I had any control over my arms or legs.

"And I'm supposed to show my face at school tomorrow?" I asked.

"It wasn't that bad," Russ said.

This, coming from a kid wearing a periodic table T-shirt with a huge chunk of mushroom jammed in his braces.

"You've got to be kidding me."

"No. I mean, it didn't look that bad at the time." Russ squinted at the TV. "But the slow motion isn't doing you any favors."

"I can't believe this is happening."

"I doubt anybody even saw it," Dad said. "Seriously, O, how many of your friends watch the nightly news?"

I didn't think *anybody* I knew watched the stupid news,

but the next day, practically every kid in the hallway either laughed, impersonated my arms spinning around while I looked totally lost, or worse, both.

All I wanted to do was hide.

It was the most embarrassing moment of my life.

And I couldn't really blame Dante Powers. Because he hadn't even tried to humiliate me with his playing or make me look like a loser. No, he was just doing his own thing. He was an awesome player, so he played awesome. It was as simple as that.

But Mitch and Marcus were another story, and I was pretty ticked off at both of them.

They'd had each other's backs every second of the game, and when they weren't feeding each other the ball and making baskets, they were doubling up on Dante and the rest of the Huskies, making each other look like superstars.

🏀   🏀   🏀

In the cafeteria, I met up with Nate, Paul, and Nicky Chu at our usual table.

"Incoming!" Nate warned, and we all ducked our heads.

About half a second later, three slices of unidentified lunch meat slapped the wall next to us, then slid down it and disappeared under the table.

All that was left was a trail of shiny slime.

"Seriously gross," Paul groaned.

We all looked over at the far corner, where we knew the eighth graders were sitting.

Sure enough, they were laughing at us.

"Hey, is that Mitch and Marcus?" Nate asked.

It was! They were sitting with the eighth graders and shrugging at us, like they hadn't been able to stop the food from flying our way.

"So *that's* where they spend their lunch hour," I muttered.

"They've been eating over there every day," Chris said. "Haven't you guys noticed?"

"The eighth graders invited them to sit over there?" Nate asked.

"They must have," Chris said with a shrug.

"Traitors," I muttered, taking a bite of my turkey sandwich.

"*They* didn't throw it," Paul said.

"So? They shouldn't be sitting with those guys, anyway."

Nicky Chu rolled his eyes. "Are you saying that if the eighth graders invited *you* to sit at their table, you'd turn them down?"

"Definitely," I said, sounding way more sure than I felt.

"Yeah, right," Nate said, laughing.

"All I know," Nicky Chu said, "is we owe the Matthews twins, big-time."

"What?" I gasped, losing half of a mouthful of turkey.

"Say it, don't spray it," Paul said, wiping chunks off his shirt.

"Owe them for what?" I asked, looking at each of them and their stupid gelled hair. "Coming up with a new hairstyle?"

"No, saving our tails at yesterday's game," Nicky said, shrugging.

"*Dude*, we lost," I reminded him.

"Yeah, by seventeen points. It could have been a total blowout."

"Seventeen points isn't a blowout?" I gasped. "On what planet?"

Nicky sighed. "All I'm saying is Dante Powers could have made that game seriously embarrassing."

I felt a quick blast of hope. Maybe none of the Pioneers had seen me on TV!

"Exactly," Nate said. "Thanks to Mitch and Marcus, we left Hogarth with some dignity."

"Well, most of us did," Paul snickered. "Did anybody catch Owen on channel twelve?"

"Don't even, Paul," I snapped, before anyone else could say a word.

"It was classic," he continued, chuckling. "The way your arms kept swinging when there was nothing there? It cracked me up."

"I didn't think it was funny," Chris said.

I was glad somebody had my back until I realized he wasn't finished.

"It was *hilarious*."

"Thanks a lot," I muttered.

At that moment, I felt someone smack the back of my head. I spun around, ready to tear them apart, but there was nobody there.

"Oh, man," Nate said, shaking his head. "That's over the top."

I didn't know what he was talking about until I felt the wet meat slide past my ear and into my lap.

"You've got to be kidding me," I muttered, feeling my face get hot.

I'd had it.

I didn't even bother looking at the eighth graders. I dropped my sandwich on the table and looked for something, anything I could use.

"What are you doing?" Nicky Chu asked, as I started digging around in my lunch bag.

"Bad idea," Paul said when I pulled out a container of chocolate pudding. "*Really* bad idea."

I opened the Baggie Mom used for my sandwich and dumped my pudding into it. I scraped every bit out of the cup with my spoon and smiled.

"Owen," Chris warned.

I sealed it *most* of the way.

Before my teammates could stop me, I stood up and chucked the bag as hard as I could, watching it whip through the air toward its target.

Finally, the Twinvaders were going down!

"Yes!" I whispered when it flew over the second-to-last table and into the aisle where . . .

Splat!

It hit my brother in the head.

I froze, totally shocked. And when the whole student body turned to see who'd thrown it, there I was, with guilt all over my face.

Which was probably better than pudding.

"Sorry, Russ," I said so quietly I barely even heard myself.

I couldn't see whether he was glaring at me because the chocolate goop covered both lenses of his glasses.

He didn't say a word as he turned and walked toward the bathroom. A couple of his Masters of the Mind friends followed him, and I definitely saw *their* glares.

"Geez, Owen. What did you do that for?" Paul asked, as soon as the cafeteria was buzzing with conversation again.

"It was an accident," I snapped.

"An accident?" Chris asked.

"I mean hitting Russ was an accident, and—"

Before I had a chance to say anything else, one of the cafeteria ladies was standing next to me. She didn't look happy.

That made two of us.

Three, if I counted Russ.

I honestly couldn't believe my luck, but after a whole afternoon of worrying about how mad Russ was, he forgave me on the way home. As soon as I explained what had happened and what I'd been trying to do, he nodded and said, "I understand."

I knew I didn't deserve his forgiveness, but I was very happy to have it.

"I'll bet Mom and Dad get a call from the principal," I told him. "I'm gonna be toast."

"Nope," he said, shaking his head. "I went to the office after I cleaned up and told them it was an accident. Luckily Mrs. Meadows hadn't actually seen it happen."

I let out a huge sigh of relief. "Thank you, Russ."

"You're my brother," he said with a shrug.

"Yeah, but—"

"I'm not saying it was a good idea, because it was terrible."

"I know," I said, and sighed. Russ couldn't hurt a fly. Not even a pair of superannoying identical flies that were just *begging* to be swatted.

He was a much better person than I was.

"The aerodynamics were awful," he said.

"What?" I asked, surprised.

"You would have been better off leaving it in the cup with the lid off."

"But I—"

"Throwing that bag was like trying to aim a jellyfish

when you could have been firing . . . I don't know, a shark."
He nodded once, like that made perfect sense. "Yeah, what
you needed was a shark."

I was totally stunned.

I had no idea what he was talking about, but I could tell
he was on my side.

And that was enough.

When I sat down to watch the Blazers game with Dad that
night, I was still ticked off at the Twinvaders.

All week, I'd been trying to come up with ideas for how
to take them out of the basketball equation, and I still didn't
know what to do.

I'd brainstormed ways to get them kicked off the team,
and finding a way to turn the rest of the guys against
them, but it was really hard. I knew exactly what result I
wanted, but I couldn't come up with any real *plans* to make
it happen.

"Popcorn?" Dad asked, handing me the bowl.

The hot, buttery goodness was almost enough to turn
my attitude around. Almost. I took a handful and shoved it
into my mouth.

"The Blazers take on Memphis," Dad said. "This could be
a tough game."

I nodded, still chewing.

My favorite team was on the ball from the second the ref tossed it.

DeShawn Williams passed to Jenkins, who booked it down the court faster than anyone in the Western Conference. Then he slipped past Jim Masters and floated through the air for a solid dunk.

Yes!

The Grizzlies' guard dribbled to the center line, but the second he crossed it, Carl Walters came out of nowhere and stole the ball.

Yes, again!

"Nice move," Dad said, reaching for the popcorn.

In fact, it was *so* nice, I forgot about the twins.

That is, until Russ joined us on the couch.

He watched for a few minutes, catching up on what he'd missed.

"Where's Antoine Marchand?" he asked, squinting at the screen.

"On the bench," Dad said. "Torn ACL."

That had to be the worst injury on the planet. No one ever knew how long guys would be out when it happened to them.

Wait a second.

I leaned back in my seat as the plan of all plans dropped right into my lap and I smiled.

After the game, I spent an hour hunched over a notebook in my room, drawing all kinds of awesome diagrams.

I came up with a bunch of different ideas for taking out at least one Twinvader, and soon my notebook was filled with all kinds of possible accidents.

When it was time for bed, I made a pit stop in Russ's room before I brushed my teeth.

"I have an idea," I told him, clutching the notebook to my chest.

"An idea about what?"

"The Matthews twins."

His eyebrows rose, as if he was interested, and I liked seeing that. Some of my plans would take the strength of at least two people. I looked at Russ's toothpick arms. Well, one and a half would work.

I opened the notebook and started slowly flipping through the pages so he could see my diagrams.

"I'm thinking one of them could tear his ACL."

"What?" Russ gasped.

"That would split them up, so they couldn't dominate the team."

Russ checked out the drawing I'd done of a catapult. It was old-school, but I knew it would work.

He turned to the next page, which showed one of the brothers with his foot twisted in a big hole he'd stepped into while trying to outrun a vicious dog.

Russ's eyes bugged out. "Are you insane?"

"I know we don't have a dog, but—"

He frowned. "That's not the problem here."

"Okay, I also don't know exactly how to build the catapult, but there are probably instructions online and—"

"Really? What about this piano, dropping off a cliff?" he asked.

"We could use a pulley and—"

"Are you trying to kill the Road Runner, Owen?" He shook his head. "And just so you know, dropping a piano on someone would do more than tear his ACL."

"We don't have to use that idea. I have tons more."

He shook his head. "And they're *all* insane."

"Okay, okay," I reasoned. "What if we tried for something a little less serious, like maybe a sprain or something?"

"We?"

"Well, yeah."

Russ frowned. "You really want to hurt the twins, don't you?"

"No, just *one* of them. And it isn't about *hurting* him as much as *benching* him." I saw the way he was staring at me, like I was some kind of a monster. "What?"

"I can't believe you'd hurt someone to get more time on the court."

"I didn't say we *had* to hurt him, Russ."

He turned the page to a drawing of a Twinvader in a full body cast. "Really?"

"Okay, I get your point. It doesn't have to be superserious.

We could set up some kind of really small accident, with no major damage. You know all kinds of physics stuff, so I'm sure we could come up with a good plan together."

Russ shook his head. "Why don't we just push one of them down the stairs?"

I grinned. "Yes! Now you're talking! Simple, quick and—"

"I'm *kidding*!" Russ snapped. "No, 'kidding' is the wrong word because this isn't funny."

"Geez. Relax, Russ."

"No, I won't. I don't like this whole sabotage idea at all. Why can't you and I just practice together more, so we'll play like they do?"

I shook my head. "Do you know how long that would take?"

"I don't care how long, Owen. That isn't the point."

Wasn't Masters of the Mind supposed to be all about thinking outside the box?

"Look. I'm just trying to fix this mess and get more court time for you and me."

He frowned even more. "That doesn't make it right, Owen." He paused for a second, then gave me a serious look. "Remember the Nikes."

"I remember," I muttered as I headed to the bathroom to brush my teeth.

While the toothpaste foamed up and dripped out of my mouth, I thought about how Russ had looked when he found out I'd dumped his beloved shoes in the school Dumpster.

I spat out the toothpaste and rinsed my mouth before walking to my bedroom.

All the basketball stuff on the walls looked awesome, but the posters, ticket stubs, books, and photos only made me feel worse.

Maybe I *was* some kind of a monster.

But I couldn't help it that basketball was my life and that all I'd wanted to do for as long as I could remember was to be out there. Winning.

And it seemed like everything was working against me.

But, as I lay on my bed, I realized that Russ was right. My plans would work only in cartoons, and maybe not even then.

I'd just have to buck up, work even harder, and practice more.

As tempting as it was, I couldn't hurt Mitch or Marcus.

As it turned out, though, I didn't have to.

Square Root

I was so busy thinking about the math test I'd be taking in last period and the fact that Owen had turned into a maniac, I didn't really notice the buzz of conversation in the hallway when I arrived at school.

I also didn't notice it during recess, when Nitu and I ran through some practice problems.

But at lunch, there was only one topic on the table, and it wasn't airborne meat.

"It's his collarbone, I think," Chris said, sounding like he was announcing the death of a beloved pet.

"I heard it was his elbow," Nate said through the crunch of a Rice Krispies Treat.

"Come on, how do you break an elbow?" Paul scoffed.

"What are you guys talking about?" I asked, pulling my sandwich out of its bag. Peanut butter again.

But before anyone could answer me, I saw exactly who they were talking about.

M&M walked into the cafeteria together, and one of them was wearing a bright-orange cast on his arm.

I'm sure my eyes widened to twice their usual size while I did my best not to look at Owen.

I cleared my throat. "Uh, which one is it?" I asked the table.

"Does it matter?" Nate asked.

"Well, it's—"

"Whichever one it is, we've lost half of the most awesome basketball duo in Lewis and Clark history."

"That might be a bit of an exaggeration," I said, glancing at Owen.

My brother didn't say a word. He just shrugged.

It didn't escape my attention that within twelve hours of Owen planning to harm Mitch or Marcus, one of them was most definitely hurt.

I raised an eyebrow at my twin, like a silent question. I wasn't sure I wanted to know the answer, but it didn't matter because Owen wasn't looking at me anymore.

Was he responsible?

Four-letter elements: gold, iron, zinc, lead . . . I glanced at the bright-orange cast. And *neon.*

I wanted to believe that Owen was past all the jealousy

over basketball, but after our conversation last night, I wasn't sure anymore.

I closed my eyes.

Five-letter elements: argon, radon, xenon . . .

"How did you do it?" a voice asked.

My eyes popped open, sure that someone at the table was onto Owen and his plan. But what I saw was the orange cast at the edge of the table.

I breathed a sigh of relief.

"Mitch and I were playing HORSE last night," the twin said, so I knew for sure he was Marcus. "Things got a little rough, and—"

"He broke your arm?" Chris asked.

Marcus shrugged. "Not exactly. I tripped over a garden hose and fell on a rock. Then, *crack*."

We all winced at the same time.

"Can you play?" Chris asked.

Marcus stared at him like it was the dumbest question he'd ever heard. "Uh, not right now."

"Bummer," Chris said with a sigh.

"I'll still be out there," Mitch said.

The guys all nodded, but I could tell they were wondering the same thing I was: How could one of them possibly pose as much of a threat as two?

$$\times \quad \div \quad +$$

The math test turned out to be a breeze, and when the bell rang, Nitu and I left the classroom together.

"It looks like the Pioneers have lost a player," she said.

"Yes," I said quietly. "It's too bad."

"Is it really?" she asked. "I mean, judging by the way you were talking about those two, I thought you might be happy about it."

"Really?" I asked, surprised. I thought I'd kept my feelings pretty well hidden from the Masters.

"You were jealous."

"Maybe," I agreed. "But that doesn't mean I wanted to see someone get *hurt*." Not Marcus, anyway. He was the nice one.

She must have seen the truth in my expression, because she patted me on the back. "It's not your fault, Russell."

✖   ÷   ✚

At practice that afternoon, Coach Baxter was obviously disappointed when he saw the cast.

"I'd heard rumors." He sighed and asked, "How long are you out for?"

"It depends on how it heals," Marcus said. "At least six weeks."

I heard a couple of the Pioneers groan.

"*Hmm.*" Coach folded his gigantic arms over his chest. "Well, we'll still have some season left in six weeks," he reminded the team. "Now, let's get warmed up."

If I were Marcus Matthews, I would have taken the opportunity to relax on the bench during the absolute worst part of practice.

But I wasn't Marcus Matthews.

As I jogged around the gym, struggling to maintain a decent pace, I watched the Matthews twins run in perfect unison.

Even with an injury, Marcus had better form than I did.

"I can't believe he's *running*," I whispered to Owen, as he passed me.

He shrugged. "There's nothing wrong with his legs."

The way he said it made me wonder if he wished there was.

As we worked through our warm-up drills, Marcus did everything that didn't require the use of his broken arm. But near the end of practice, he was stuck on the bench for the scrimmage.

"How does it feel?" I asked, as I sat next to him and waited to be subbed in.

"Lame." He sighed, then glanced at me. "You mean not being able to play, right?"

"No, I meant your arm. How does it feel?"

"Sore," he said, shrugging. "Awkward, uncomfortable, and totally frustrating."

"Tell me how you really feel," I joked.

He didn't crack a smile. "I just did."

Before I could say anything else, he pulled a notebook

out from under the bench and flipped it open to a blank page.

"Homework?" I asked.

He shook his head but didn't answer me. Instead, he bent over the book and started writing. He would watch Mitch for a couple of minutes, then scribble something on the page.

"What are you doing?" I asked.

"Taking notes," he said, like it was the most obvious thing in the world.

"Notes on what?"

"His playing," he said with a shrug.

"What do you mean?" I asked. I'd never seen anyone but the sports reporter from our school newspaper taking basketball notes before.

"It's what my dad usually does. At games, you know?"

I nodded, but I didn't know at all. "Why?"

He turned to face me. "So we can go over the action together when we get home. Then we work on improvements."

The last thing I wanted to do when I got home from a Pioneers game was dissect it. Either we won or we lost. Either we played well or we didn't.

And M&M *always* played well. What kind of improvements could they possibly need?

"Does he do it all the time?" I asked, glad that my own parents simply appeared at the games and cheered us on.

"When he's in town. He's working in New Orleans right now. Since I'm benched, I might as well do it for him."

I only watched about half of what was happening on the court because I was trying to figure out Marcus's notes. Between the scrawled words, diagrams, and grunts, it was hard to tell exactly what he was tracking. And whatever it was happened to be complicated enough that his page looked more like notes from a high-school physics class than a simple middle-school scrimmage.

"Russell!" Coach shouted. His tone let me know that it wasn't the first time he'd said my name. "You're up."

I ran out onto the court, stopping only to retie my shoelaces.

"Double knots, Russ," Owen said, for what must have been the four hundredth time since I'd joined the Pioneers.

Coach blew his whistle, and seconds later I was running down the court, checking over my shoulder to watch Nate's progress with the ball.

"I'm open!" Owen shouted. Nate threw a bounce pass right to him.

Owen managed to get the ball a few feet closer to the net but not close enough to take a shot.

Mitch was guarding me and I was worried I'd never be able to shake him off. But to my surprise, one quick spin was all it took to find myself open.

"Over here!" I shouted to Owen, who passed me the ball.

I dribbled even more carefully than usual, knowing how easily Mitch would be able to steal the ball.

But he didn't.

I did my best to hurry down the court and when I was within range, I took a shot.

"Nice!" Owen called, as the ball dropped through the net.

I turned to see where my guard was. Mitch was mouthing something to Marcus, who held his notebook in the air, as if anyone other than Superman could read it from twenty feet away.

"Let's keep our heads in the game," Coach said. "Matthews, I need you to stay focused."

Mitch nodded and shot his brother a frustrated look.

The next time I had the ball, I couldn't feel Mitch breathing down my neck, so I took off down the court. As soon as I heard his footsteps behind me, I passed to Owen, who wasn't quite ready for it. He stumbled, but managed to catch the ball and pass it to Nicky Chu for a basket.

The opposing team scored a couple of times, but then it was Nicky Chu with a beautiful layup, followed by a three-pointer by me.

It was, as Owen would say, "nothing but net," as the ball swished.

I knew it had only been a matter of minutes and it was only a practice scrimmage, but it seemed like the Pioneers were playing like a real team again. It felt amazing!

For the rest of practice, Coach Baxter shouted words of encouragement and complimented us on our playing.

Except for Mitch, that is.

He seemed to be totally distracted from the game while

most of his attention was focused on the bench. Marcus tried to help him by cheering him on, flashing complicated hand signals and holding up his notebook, but none of his efforts helped.

Coach Baxter let Mitch take a break on the bench, so he sat next to his twin and watched the rest of us play.

At first, they looked like a couple of mismatched bookends, one with a cast and one without. But when I looked closer, I saw that their expressions were exactly the same.

They both looked miserable.

$$\times \quad \div \quad +$$

I walked home from school with Owen and Chris that afternoon, and it wasn't long before the topic turned to our injured list.

"I can't believe Mitch is out for six weeks," Chris said, shaking his head.

"Marcus," I corrected.

"What?" he asked, looking confused.

"It's Marcus who's injured."

"Oh," Chris said, shrugging it off. "Whatever."

I tuned the two of them out during the rest of the walk home, distracted by what Chris had said. Well, more about how he said it than the words themselves, really.

The Matthews twins were two separate people, whether they were alike or not.

I kicked a stone ahead of me on the sidewalk, thinking about how jealous I'd been of their amazing closeness.

I'd desperately wanted Owen and me to be in sync and to feel that bond. But would I like it if we were so similar and so close that no one could tell us apart?

I thought about the math and science certificates I'd won, and how it had felt to stand on the stage and receive them. I thought about the success of the Masters of the Mind team and how amazing it was that they had chosen me for team captain.

How would I feel if I overheard someone talking about Owen's math skills, knowing they were really talking about mine? And how would he feel if the kids high-fived me in the hallway for plays he had made during a basketball game?

I didn't have to think for too long to know we would both hate it.

$$\times \quad \div \quad +$$

I went grocery shopping with Mom on the weekend and I saw M&M ahead of us in line at Safeway. I noticed that wearing the cast meant that Marcus couldn't part his hair quite so perfectly anymore, so the brothers had stopped looking exactly the same.

I didn't say anything to them, but I watched as they helped their mom unload their cart. Mitch dumped everything on the conveyor belt at once while Marcus lined up all the boxed items in a strange order. I would have gone from tallest to shortest or something like that, but his clusters of boxes were all different sizes. It wasn't until the cashier started bagging that I realized he'd grouped his boxes to perfectly fill every corner of a standard paper bag.

The cashier smiled at him as she loaded layer after layer with ease. She didn't have to make a single adjustment.

"Smart," I murmured.

"What, honey?" Mom asked.

"Nothing," I said.

But it was something. Something very interesting.

$$\times \quad \div \quad +$$

I thought I had a pretty good understanding of the twins' personalities off the court, but before Marcus broke his arm, I hadn't noticed that they assumed different roles when they hit the hardwood. Strangely enough, when it came to basketball, *Marcus* was the more aggressive brother. The more I watched, the more obvious it was that Marcus was the one who'd always found openings where they shouldn't have been. Marcus made the shots that seemed impossible.

It was as though he'd linked geometry with basketball. He'd been the one to find the awkward angles and make them work. He came up with the plays that no one saw coming.

When it was time to scrimmage, I sat next to Marcus

and watched his note taking until I had some idea of what he was seeing. And when I figured out his shorthand writing, it all made sense.

He was the creative one.

And that gave me something to seriously think about.

The Upset

I won't say it was a disaster that one of the Twinvaders broke his arm because that would be a total lie.

It was a *miracle*.

With him out of the picture, I had a second chance at having an awesome season and there was nothing wrong with that.

Nothing.

Any time a Pioneer got hurt, I stepped up my game. I knew a good opportunity when I saw one, and I wasn't going to miss out.

I tackled drills with a little more zip than usual. I ran faster, passed harder, and shot better, all so Coach Baxter could see that we didn't need those guys, anyway.

And everything was going really awesome . . . except

that Russ looked like he was starting to actually have fun hanging out with the wounded one on the bench.

I honestly didn't know what the deal was with my brother. I'm pretty sure he felt sorry for the guy, which was totally wrong. You couldn't feel sorry for the *enemy*.

You just couldn't.

On our next game day, I woke up ready for action. Finally, the court would belong to the real Pioneers again. No more doubling up by Mitch and Marcus. No more opening minutes on the bench.

And as far as winning streaks went, I knew for a fact that we'd be starting a new one.

I walked to school with Chris, who still dribbled his ball everywhere he went.

"You do that inside the house, too?" I asked, knowing there was no way my mom would let that happen.

"Only in the hallway and the kitchen," he said. "Everything else is carpet."

"Is it helping?"

"The dribbling?" He thought for a second. "Yeah, I think so."

"I guess we'll find out this afternoon."

"The Gresham Gophers," he said. "I heard they've got a good lineup this year."

"So do we," I told him, lifting my hand for a high five.

His palm slapped mine, but he wasn't smiling. "You think we can do it without the twins?"

I laughed. "You've *got* the twins, man. The Evans twins."

"No, I mean the—"

"I know who you mean," I interrupted. I didn't even want to hear their name. "But we don't need those guys."

Chris stopped dribbling. "Are you kidding me?"

"No. We were fine without them for *years*, Chris."

"Yeah, but they're so good."

"So are we," I said with a shrug. "We were in the middle of a winning streak when they got here, and look what happened. The streak ended."

He looked at me like I wasn't making sense. "But that was because of Dante Powers."

"Hey," I said, getting ticked off. "The winning streak starts again today, without the Matthews twins."

"Well, one of them will be playing."

"I *know*."

Like I wanted to be reminded of that.

Classes went by superfast, probably because I wasn't paying attention. I knew that would come back to bite me in the butt later, like when we took our next test or something, but I was having too much fun daydreaming to stop.

While Mrs. Barber talked about fractions, I pictured myself scoring the winning shot against Gresham, right at the buzzer. I didn't want the game to be *that* close, but I liked imagining the big moment, anyway.

While Mr. Hathaway explained the meaning of a short story I forgot to read for homework, I imagined the Pioneers making their way toward Gresham's basket, no-look passes all the way.

At lunch, I met the guys at our usual table and was kind of disappointed to see Mitch and Marcus sitting at the far end.

"What are they doing here?" I asked Russ. "Did the eighth graders ditch them?"

"No, I invited them to join us."

"You what?" I choked.

"They're on our team, Owen."

"Yeah, you keep saying that."

"Because it's true," he told me, then took a bite of his apple. It was so juicy, I got sprayed in the face.

There was no point in trying to convince Russ that he sounded completely crazy, so I didn't bother. I just dug into my own lunch bag and started eating.

I didn't like thinking about how important the brothers had become to the team. And I definitely didn't like thinking that we stood a better chance of losing without both of them playing.

Even if we did play, well, like *us*, we still wouldn't be playing like *them*.

I shook my head, knowing that kind of thinking wasn't going to help at all.

I needed to get back in the game . . . before the game.

I saw the Gresham Middle School bus parked in front of the school when I ran downstairs at the end of the day.

On their way to our front door were a bunch of Gophers wearing matching green and gray warm-ups. I checked them out through the window.

They looked taller than most of the teams we played, and kind of . . . older.

I jumped down the last few stairs and ran to the locker room. I was the first one there, and I was already suited up and tying my laces by the time Nicky Chu and Russ showed up.

"This is gonna be rough," Nicky said.

"You saw them, too, huh?"

"Who?" he asked.

"The Gophers."

He looked confused. "No."

"Then why is it gonna be rough?"

"Uh, news flash, Owen. We're down a man."

"We'll be fine," I told him, wishing I didn't have to convince everybody of that.

I headed for the court to warm up so I'd be ready to outplay . . . well, everyone.

I dribbled the ball for a while, even through the legs as I walked toward center. I looked at the scoreboard I'd lit up a hundred times before and then glanced into the stands, where I knew our fans would be rooting for us.

I took a deep breath, filling my lungs with gymnasium air.

I loved knowing that we had a better record than the Gophers. I could already taste the win, and it tasted awesome, like a double cheeseburger and fries.

I dribbled over to the free throw line, my favorite warm-up spot. I bounced the ball twice, then bent my knees. I bounced it again and moved my head from side to side, to loosen up my neck.

Another two bounces and a knee bend.

"Are you going to shoot, or what?" a voice asked from behind me.

I spun around and saw the twin in the orange cast.

"I'm warming up," I muttered.

"It looks more like you're warming up for a warm-up to warm up."

"Very funny," I said, rolling my eyes. "I've only got a few minutes before the game, so if you don't mind . . . ," I said, then waited as he walked back to the bench.

He had that stupid notebook with him, and when he sat down, he whipped it open and started scribbling in it.

Whatever.

I turned back to the basket, finally ready to take my shot.

With a loud *bang*, the gym door swung open and the Gophers poured in so fast I wished our team was called the Exterminators.

I quickly took my shot.

After all that buildup, I missed.

"Ouch," Nate said, dribbling past me for a nice layup.

I grabbed the ball and walked back to my position to take another shot.

Swish.

"Nothing but net," I told him.

"Cool," he said, going in for another one.

I'd barely had time to bounce the ball when the rest of the Pioneers came out of the locker room. Everyone looked nervous, but I knew for a fact that once we heard the ref's whistle, everything would fall into place.

Just like the old days.

I glanced at the bench, where the healthy twin was sitting next to his brother and looking over the notebook.

For once, they were talking to each other with their voices instead of their minds.

The whole time the guys and I were warming up, they sat on that bench and studied the notebook, like it was the most interesting thing on the planet.

By the time Coach blew his whistle for a huddle, the healthy one was still wearing his hoodie and hadn't even touched a ball.

Fine with me. The less prepared he was, the better all of us would look.

I knew things were going my way when Coach put me in as a forward and Russ at center. And rounding out the front line was Paul.

Not a Matthews twin on the hardwood!

I loved it.

Gresham took possession at the tip-off, but Nate stole the ball in about two seconds flat.

We weren't on fire yet, but we had a spark.

That spark caught flame when Nate dribbled all the way down the court and threw a bounce pass to Russ, who happened to be in perfect position for one of his trademark three-pointers!

We were officially back in business!

For the next three minutes, we were up and down the court more times than I could count, and the Pioneers racked up a quick eleven points.

"Yes!" I said, shaking a fist in the air.

But the excitement didn't last long.

Paul was dribbling down the court, a blur of blue and white, trailed by two Gophers who were desperate to catch him.

He was almost to the basket when he tripped over his own feet and fell to the ground.

The ball rolled toward the sidelines and I waited for him to jump up and grab it, but he just lay there.

"Uh-oh," I whispered.

"Did he twist his ankle?" Russ asked. "It looked like he twisted it."

"No, he just tripped. He's fine," I told him, hoping I was right.

Paul sat up, his face whiter than the soles of his Nikes, and clutched his ankle.

"He doesn't look fine," Russ said.

Coach Baxter jogged out onto the court where Paul sat, holding his foot like it was going to fall off his leg.

The rest of us held our breath as Coach talked to him while pressing on different parts of his foot and ankle.

Paul gritted his teeth, then yowled in pain.

"No way," I whispered.

Coach and the ref helped him up onto one foot as he hopped off the court.

"This doesn't look good," Chris said.

"Not at all," I said, rubbing my forehead.

Everything had been so perfect! The Twinvaders were on the bench, the original Pioneers were rocking the court . . . and now Paul was hurt?

The game was held for about five minutes while Paul was taken to the doctor. When he turned back to look at us, there was nothing the rest of us could do but wave and nod as he left.

Shoot!

I had a feeling I knew what was going to happen next.

Coach Baxter decided to put the healthy twin in.

Even though we'd been scrimmaging with him all week at practice, he didn't look right. It took me a minute to realize I'd never seen him in uniform by himself.

"He looks weird alone," I whispered to Russ.

"He's not alone," Russ said. "He's with us."

"Whatever," I said, shaking my head. If Russ wanted to live in some messed-up alternate universe, that was his own business.

The ref blew his whistle and the game was on again.

One of the Gophers dribbled up to the basket and went in for a layup, but Russ was ready to block the shot with a single hand.

"Denied!" a bunch of girls screamed from the bleachers.

I took off down the court, ready to put some points on the board, but right when I got to the net, a Gopher popped up out of nowhere. I couldn't get past him or through him, so I looked for help.

"Matthews is open!" Chris shouted.

There had to be somebody else. If I wasn't going to score, I wanted a real Pioneer to do it.

I bounced the ball and looked at the shot clock. Three seconds left.

I checked over both shoulders and there was nobody to pass to.

Nobody but a Matthews brother.

I had no choice.

I tossed the ball to him and he caught it easily enough. But that was all he did.

Seriously. He just stood there!

"Shoot!" I yelled, as two of the Gophers made their move, but it was too late. They'd already stolen the ball.

"What was that?" I asked the twin, smirking as we jogged toward the center line.

He didn't say anything. In fact, he totally ignored me.

I would have ignored him, too, but for the rest of the quarter, every time I had the ball, he was my only option. And every time I threw it to him, the kid totally froze.

It was awesome!

"What's his deal?" I asked Russ during a break in the action.

"I don't know. Maybe he just needs some time to warm up."

"Warm up?" I laughed. "The quarter's almost over and he totally stinks."

I couldn't have dreamed up a better situation!

"And we still have three more quarters to play," Russ said, fixing his glasses.

"Totally not the point," I told him.

I wondered if the guy would get his act together soon.

Lucky for me, the answer was no.

Secondary Data

I don't know whether it was more painful to watch Mitch Matthews struggle on the court or to watch pure happiness take over my brother's face while he did it.

Coach Baxter had pulled me out to rest, since I still hadn't built up the kind of stamina my teammates had. I could handle a few minutes of play at a time, but not much more.

Owen, on the other hand, suddenly looked like he'd had a long nap and could play for hours.

I'd seen his energy level pick up the first time Mitch lost the ball for us, and he'd seemed happier every time Mitch made a bad pass or missed a shot, which was actually pretty often.

Marcus was the exact opposite. With every mistake Mitch made, he jumped up from the bench or shouted advice that was too late for his brother to use. Then he scrawled notes in his book as he shook his head.

"I'm sure he'll be fine," I said.

Marcus glanced over at me. "I hope so."

"He will," I said with a confident nod. "Don't worry."

Marcus offered me a shy smile. "Thanks, Russell."

At halftime, the Matthews twins left the gym to talk while Owen grabbed a bottle of water from the cooler and sat next to me on the bench.

"You're playing well," I told him.

"Thanks."

I waited for him to say something about Mitch, but he didn't.

"It looks like Mitch is having a tough time out there," I said.

"That's for sure," he agreed, laughing. "The guy can't get it together *at all*."

"It's too bad," I said quietly.

"For him, maybe, but not for the rest of us. The Pioneers are back!"

"And trailing by six," I pointed out.

Owen rolled his eyes. "It's only halftime, Russ. We'll get it back."

"I hope so," I told him.

But we didn't.

The third quarter was full of sloppy plays and bad judgment. The fourth was even worse.

I was back in the game when we had three minutes left on the clock.

Owen had the ball and was dribbling down the court faster than I'd ever seen him, his face shiny with perspiration.

"I'm open!" I called. I waited for the pass, which was perfect. So was my position—I didn't have to move an inch before I took the jump shot.

The ball teetered on the rim before falling through the net.

"Three points!" Owen shouted, already racing back toward our basket. "Let's keep it up, guys!"

Nate scored a couple more times with some nice layups. When Nicky Chu was fouled, he made both of his baskets for another two points.

But the Gophers were scoring, too, and we couldn't keep up.

At the two-minute mark, Owen was hit in the face by a flying elbow and given two free throws.

I watched as he lined up the first shot and bent his knees before bouncing the ball once. He straightened and threw it.
Thunk.

It bounced off the rim and the crowd groaned.

Owen bobbed up and down on his toes a few times to loosen up and took another shot.

This one sailed right in.

"Yes!" he said, pumping his fist hard.

We had twenty-three seconds left when Mitch Matthews dribbled down the court, surrounded by Gophers. He spun around to shake off the player who had a grip on the back of his jersey and took the shot.

The ball bounced off the corner of the backboard just as the buzzer sounded.

And with that, we officially lost.

Our new winning streak had turned into a losing streak.

I followed the rest of the guys into the locker room, listening as they tried to cheer each other up.

"Are you happy now?" I asked Owen, when he opened the locker next to me.

"What? No."

"You got what you wanted," I reminded him.

He didn't say anything but I knew from his expression that he was trying to hold back a smile.

✕   ÷   ✚

I ate lunch in Mr. Hollis's room one afternoon, tired of watching my brother gloat at the lunch table. As I bit into my ham sandwich, I tried to ignore the word "jerk" as it flashed in my head over and over again.

Why couldn't Owen root *for* the team instead of rooting *against* the Matthews brothers?

"You're in here early," a voice said, from the doorway.

I looked up to see Marcus, alone.

"I'm just taking a break from the cafeteria." I quickly added, "It's too noisy in there."

"I know what you mean," he said, walking into the room and setting his books on the table next to mine.

"Where's Mitch?" I asked, surprised to see him alone.

"The cafeteria. I left to see the school nurse."

"Are you okay?" I asked, glancing at his cast.

"Yeah. It's just that my arm gets really itchy, and she has a special scratcher I can poke down there."

"Cool," I said, nodding.

"Have you finished your homework assignment?"

I couldn't help laughing. No one had asked me that for years. "It's done."

"Mine, too." He pulled a book out of his bag and flipped it open. "Want to play a word game until the bell?"

"Sure," I said, smiling. I was pretty good at word games and looked forward to maybe showing off a little.

"It's an etymology game," he said, then glanced at me. "You know what that means, right?"

"Etymology? Sure, it's where a word comes from."

"And why," he said. "For example, the word 'ballot'? It comes from the Italian word for a pebble. Italians used to vote by putting a pebble into whichever box they chose."

"Interesting," I said, and meant it.

He looked down at the page. "Want to take a guess at 'escape'?"

I thought about it for a moment. "It sounds like it might be French?"

He shook his head and smiled. "That's what I would have guessed, too. It's Latin. Want to guess the why?"

I nodded, already liking the way this game stretched my brain in new directions.

After a full minute, I'd tossed out a few ideas but hadn't found the right one. "So, what is it?" I asked, excited to learn something new.

He read, "In Latin, it means, 'out of cape.' It says here that the ancient Romans would try to avoid capture by throwing off their capes when they ran."

"I like that one," I said. "It's kind of like shar-peis."

He gave me a quizzical look. "You mean those wrinkled dogs?"

"Yeah. They were bred that way in China. If they were attacked by another animal, the other animal would only be able to grab loose skin and do less damage than if it bit into the body."

"Weird," Marcus said, then smiled. "But cool."

"Let's try another one from the book," I said, totally enjoying myself.

"Okay, here's a good one. 'Regret.'"

It was a funny word to choose, because it was something I was feeling at that very moment.

If I'd given Marcus a chance at the very beginning, we could have been friends all along.

✖   ➗   ✚

Over the next couple of days, I thought a lot about Marcus Matthews. I thought about how interesting he'd turned out to be, and how he'd opened my eyes to some new ways of looking at things, like words.

I also thought about how lost he seemed without basketball.

And I knew there was something I could do about that.

It turned out I had to wait until the Pioneers' next practice to catch him alone.

We were sitting on the bench when I asked, "Have you ever heard of Masters of the Mind?"

"The team?" he asked, and when I nodded he said, "Yeah."

"We specialize in thinking outside the box."

He didn't say anything.

"So do you," I finally added.

"What?"

"You specialize in thinking outside the box."

"I do?" he asked.

"Yes. Here at practice, in math class . . . everywhere." I took a deep breath. "And we could use someone like you."

It wasn't something I'd ever really believed I'd suggest, even though Nitu had wanted me to do it. But when I took a good look at the way I was behaving, I realized I was no different from Owen. I'd been acting as if it was better to sacrifice the Masters team than to invite Marcus to be part of it.

And that was ridiculous.

"Me?" he asked, looking surprised. "For what?"

"To be on the team. We're short a member, so . . ."

I waited for him to jump at the opportunity, but he looked out at his twin instead. "You think *I'm* the guy for the team?"

"Yes."

"*Hmm*," he said, still staring at Mitch.

"What do you say?"

"I'll have to think about it."

He'd have to think about it?

As far as I could see, he had nothing else to do!

"It's a really good way to meet friends," I told him.

"Friends?"

"Yes. You know, people you hang out with—"

"I know what a friend is. I just don't need one."

"You what?"

"I have Mitch. He's my best friend."

"Oh." I considered Owen my friend, but he wasn't my *best* friend. That was Nitu. And Owen had Chris. "But now that Mitch is playing and you aren't, maybe it's a good time to look into some other activities."

He stared at me. "I play basketball."

"Yes, but not right now. What else do you like?"

He thought for a second. "We like—"

"No, not the two of you. What do *you* like?"

He looked like he'd never been asked that question before. I could see that he was struggling with the answer.

"Marcus?"

"I don't know," he said, shaking his head. "We do everything together. We always have."

He watched his brother on the court. He didn't just look uncertain, he looked lost.

I couldn't imagine being so linked to Owen that I had no opinions of my own.

"Well," I said. "I think you'd like *Masters of the Mind*."

"Really?"

"Really," I said with a firm nod. "At least think about it, okay?"

He nodded.

The Assist

Okay, it's true that I got what I wanted.

The one I'd figured out was Mitch was a total mess on the court and that meant the rest of us looked like pros.

Except for Paul, anyway.

Yes, it stunk that not all the original Pioneers were out there together, and losing wasn't the greatest, but our record was good enough that we could bounce back later.

If taking the Twinvaders down meant losing a couple of games, I was totally okay with that.

And losing a couple of games was exactly what happened next.

I practically cheered every time Mitch lost possession and every *thunk* of the ball bouncing off the rim sounded like music to me.

"Try not to look too happy," Russ muttered when we were both on the bench.

"I can't help it," I told him. "Everything is working out perfectly."

"Except that we're down eleven points."

"We'll make it up," I promised, kind of hoping we wouldn't. The more baskets Mitch missed, the more obvious it was that his lame playing was dragging us all down.

Coach called a time-out and the rest of the guys joined us on the sidelines.

"You okay out there, Mitch?" he asked.

He nodded. "Yup."

"Doesn't look like it to me," I whispered to Russ, who took a step away from me.

Touchy!

While Coach gave a pretty decent pep talk to my discouraged teammates, I watched the Twinvaders study another page in that stupid book. Marcus frantically scribbled with a pencil while Mitch nodded, like a drawing was going to help anything.

What a waste of time.

But that was okay with me. If he wanted to study sketches instead of scoring points, it would only make the rest of us look better.

In the second half, Mitch was an even bigger mess than

before. His dribbling was sloppy, his shots were garbage, and instead of getting his head in the game, he kept looking at his brother on the bench.

It was awesome.

I was walking home from school with Russ, Chris, and Nate one afternoon when Nate said, "This season is going down the tubes, fast."

"Not really," I said, smiling to myself.

"What are you talking about?" Nate asked, surprised. "We've got Marcus riding the bench, Mitch's playing is awful, and Paul's *still* out with his injury."

"Okay, so Paul wasn't supposed to get hurt, but—"

"No one was *supposed* to get hurt," Nate said.

"Yeah, yeah, I know," I told him. "But it would have been nice if only Marcus was out."

"Nice?" Chris asked, raising an eyebrow.

"You know what I mean," I said, shrugging.

I glanced at Russ, who was shaking his head like I should stop talking.

"No, I don't," Nate said. "Unless you mean that you like that one of the best players on the team is hurt and we'll never win another game . . ."

"We'll win another game," I told him, sure of it.

"I don't get you, O," Chris said, shaking his head. "We're supposed to be in this together."

"Exactly," I told him. "This season is about the *original* Pioneers."

Chris looked at my brother, then back at me. "Russ isn't an original Pioneer."

"That's what I told him," Russ said.

"Look—" I started to explain, but Nate cut me off.

"No, *you* look, Owen. It doesn't matter who was here first or who joined the team partway into the season."

"They didn't even have to try out," I muttered.

"Who cares?" Nate said. "We're a team now, and it would be nice to be a *winning* team."

"Yeah, but—"

"I'm not finished," he snapped. "We need to pull this team together and forget about jealousy and all that other junk."

"I'm not jeal—"

"*Owen*," Russ said, giving me a look.

"He's right," Chris said. "If we want to have a decent season and a chance at play-offs this year, we've got to figure out a way for Mitch to play the way he used to, without his brother."

"I don't think that's—"

"Seriously, what is your problem, Owen?" Nate interrupted. "Why do you hate Mitch?"

"Hate him? I don't *hate* him."

"Yeah, right," Russ muttered.

"What did he ever do to you?" Nate demanded.

I wasn't going to say anything, but I blurted out, "It's both of them, you guys. The Matthews twins are ruining everything."

"By scoring points?" Chris asked.

"By winning games?" Nate added. "Come on, man. They helped the team *and* they're really cool guys."

That was pushing it.

"With matching haircuts," I said with a snort.

Nate shook his head, like he was disgusted. "If you can't see past the haircuts, you've got a problem, Owen."

"What, so you're best friends with them now?" I snapped.

He shrugged. "They heard me say I was having problems in math and offered to help me."

"What?"

"Me, too," Chris said. "Not math, though. English."

"You never told me that!" I gasped.

"I figured you'd flip out," Chris said, glancing at me. "And it looks like I was right."

I shook my head and tried to slow down all the thoughts that were crowding my brain. "So they offered to help you with homework. Big deal."

"It's a big deal to me," Nate said. "If I fail math, you think Coach will let me play?"

"You're not going to fail math," I said, rolling my eyes.

"Thanks to Mitch and Marcus, you're probably right."

"You really need to give them a chance, Owen," Chris said.

"A chance to what? Take over the whole universe?"

Russ sighed. "Be reasonable, O."

"Listen to the genius of the family," Nate said. "The reasonable thing to do is to help get Mitch up to speed so the Pioneers can start winning again."

I hated to admit it, but deep inside, I knew he was right. We could handle a couple of losses, but there would be no winning streaks and no play-offs waiting for us if things didn't turn around.

"Fine," I said, sighing. "So, how are we going to do that?"

"Well," Chris asked, "how did we get Russ ready for try-outs?"

"*We* didn't," I reminded him, thinking of all the time I'd spent practicing with my brother. "*I* did."

"Exactly," Chris said with a nod. "And you'll do it again."

It wasn't nearly as easy as Chris made it sound. First, I had to convince Mitch—who thought I was a total jerk and maybe he was kind of right—to practice with me.

"Why?" he asked.

"Because you stink without Marcus."

He rolled his eyes. "I meant, why do *you* want to help me?"

"To be honest, I don't," I admitted.

"What?"

"I don't want to help you. I want to help the team."

"So do I."

"I want to win."

He shrugged. "So do I."

"Yeah, but probably not as much as I do," I told him.

"This isn't a contest. We both want the exact same thing, Russell."

"I'm Owen," I reminded him.

"Sorry," he said, but not like he really meant it. "Okay, if you're willing to help me, I'm willing to practice with you."

"Awesome," I said. "My place. Nine o'clock tomorrow morning." Then I walked away, cool as could be.

"Owen?" he called after me.

"Yeah?" I asked, turning around.

"I don't know where you live."

⚫ 🏀 ⊛

The next morning, both of the Twinvaders were on my doorstep at nine sharp.

"Uh, this was just going to be a one-on-one thing," I reminded Mitch. The last thing I needed was the two of them ganging up on me.

"I know," Marcus said. "I'm here for the meeting."

"What meeting?" I asked.

"Masters of the Mind," Russ said, from behind me. "Marcus is thinking about joining."

"Masters of the Mind?" I asked.

"Try to keep up," Mitch said, smiling.

We left the two of them at my house as Mitch and I walked to the park. Neither of us spoke as we each dribbled a ball.

When we got there, I was relieved to see that the court was empty.

"So, what's the deal?" I asked. "Why do you freeze up when your brother's not around?"

"He's the only guy I've ever played with."

That didn't even make sense. "But you were on other teams, with other people."

"Sure, but we did our own thing. At practices, at home, and at games."

I thought about all the times I'd seen Mitch and Marcus off to the side at practice or hanging out together in the hallways. I thought about how they always seemed to be on their own.

"Just like you've done here," I said.

"Yeah. We don't need anyone else."

I laughed. "You totally do."

"No, we don't."

"You do right now," I reminded him. "As long as he's out with that arm, you need the rest of us."

He was quiet for a minute. "I know you're right," he finally said, "but Marcus is the only person I trust."

"Then you're going to have to learn to trust me," I told him.

He looked me right in the eye. "And you're going to have to earn it."

"Excuse me?"

"You're the only guy on this team who wants me to fail."

How did he know that?

"And that's why I'm spending my Saturday trying to help you, right?"

"Okay, up until *yesterday* you wanted me to fail. Ever since Marcus and I got here, everyone else has been fine, but you've been acting like you don't want us on the team."

"Well . . . yeah." I thought for a second. "But I don't feel that way anymore."

"And I'm supposed to believe that?" he asked, crossing his arms.

"I want to *win*, okay?"

We stared at each other while crows cawed in the trees all around us.

"How about this?" Mitch suggested. "I'll admit that I need you and the rest of the Pioneers if you admit that you need me."

The final score from our last game flashed in my head and my answer was painful but obvious.

"I need you," I told him. "The Pioneers need you."

"And I need you, too," he said, then bounced his ball a couple of times. "Now let's do this."

So we did.

For the next two hours, I ran the same kind of drills with Mitch that I had with Russ.

The biggest change he had to make was with communication. He was so used to automatically knowing where Marcus would be and vice versa, he didn't think to shout that he was open or listen for anyone else to say that they were.

"You don't hear the guys on the court?" I asked.

"Nah, I just tune it out."

Just then, some high-school kids showed up. I wasn't sure if they'd boot us off the court, but they invited us to play instead.

"Sure," I said, "as long as me and him are on the same team."

From the second we started playing, I knew that the work we'd done all morning had been totally worth it.

Mitch and I were like . . . well, like our own kind of Twinvaders. We passed, blocked, and made shots together. The more we played, the more comfortable we got with each other. He started calling plays and I started guessing what moves he would make.

By the time the game was over, I felt like we'd been teammates for at least a couple of seasons.

And I never thought I'd ever say this, but that was . . . pretty awesome.

Whole Numbers

My Masters team was headed to Regionals in just one week, with a brand-new member. He took some convincing, but once Marcus chose to join us, he put his whole heart into the team.

Everybody loved him and the great ideas he brought to the table.

"Now that we're a team of five, I know that we are going to thrive," Nitu said at our last meeting after a particularly good brainstorming session.

"Regionals are coming soon," I said. "We win there and I'm over the moon."

"Nice one," Sara said.

The room was quiet for a few seconds, then Marcus gave us a shy smile.

"What have you got?" Jason asked.

Marcus cleared his throat. "Our chance at Regionals is great, and then we're on the road to State." He paused. "I know we deal in rationals, but why not dream of Nationals?"

I grinned.

The kid was a natural.

And I loved it.

✖   ➗   ➕

Marcus brought great ideas to the Masters team, but he had more than a few for the Pioneers, too.

When Coach Baxter took a look at his notes, he saw that Marcus had a keen eye for Mitch's strengths and weaknesses. So he asked him to watch the rest of us as well, to help pinpoint areas where *we* could use some help.

As a result, I think every single player on the team improved.

Even Owen.

We were down to the last few seconds of a game against Riverbend.

The score was tied and Nate had the ball.

He dribbled around a guard who'd had a hard time keeping up with him for the whole game. Then he passed to Owen.

My brother raced down the court, and I was sure he would go for the shot. After all, there wasn't much time left and he was in perfect position to score.

Then one of the guards made a move and almost stole the ball.

Owen remained calm, amazingly enough. He checked over his shoulder—there was nothing but Riverbend players in his sights.

"I'm open!" Mitch shouted.

Owen hesitated for a split second. It was the kind of thing only someone really close to him (like me) would notice. He took a deep breath like he'd made a tough decision.

I hoped he was about to do the right thing for the team.

And he did.

One quick bounce pass and the ball was in Mitch's hands.

A second later, it was back in the air and zooming for the basket.

We all froze in place as it rolled around the rim once, twice . . .

"Come on," Chris whispered, from next to me.

I crossed my fingers and held my breath.

After a final trip around the rim, the ball dropped through the net with the most satisfying *swish* I'd ever heard.

The Pioneers won!

Owen pumped his fist in the air and shouted, "Yes!"

I waited for him to high-five Mitch. Instead, the two of them nodded to each other and smiled.

And that was good enough.

Acknowledgments

As always, tremendous thanks to my agent, Sally Harding of the Cooke Agency, who has put up with my pesky e-mails for over ten years. And to my editor, Brett Wright at Bloomsbury, for his thoughtful direction and boundless enthusiasm.